Brave Enough

Brave Enough

Kati Gardner

Mendota Heights, Minnesota

First Edition
Third Printing, 2018

Book design by Sarah Taplin
Cover design by Sarah Taplin
Cover images by Pixabay

Flux, an imprint of North Star Editions, Inc.

Library of Congress Cataloging-in-Publication Data
Names: Gardner, Kati, author.
Title: Brave enough / Kati Gardner.
Description: First edition. | Mendota Heights, Minnesota : Flux, [2018] | Summary: The lives of Davis Channing, a cancer surviving recovering addict, and Cason Martin, a ballerina undergoing chemotherapy, intersect in a powerful way when both are struggling to survive life-threatening diseases.
Identifiers: LCCN 2018020716 (print) | LCCN 2018029496 (ebook) | ISBN 9781635830217 (ebook) | ISBN 9781635830200 (pbk. : alk. paper)
Subjects: | CYAC: Cancer—Fiction. | Drug abuse—Fiction. | Ballet dancing—Fiction.
Classification: LCC PZ7.1.G3724 (ebook) | LCC PZ7.1.G3724 Br 2018 (print) |
  DDC [Fic]—dc23
LC record available at https://lccn.loc.gov/2018020716

Flux
North Star Editions, Inc.
2297 Waters Drive
Mendota Heights, MN 55120
www.fluxnow.com

To Jason, Kennedy, and Eleanor,
You have each helped me be fearless.

Mama,
Thank you for always believing in my stories.

Camp Sunshine,
Sunshine Forever, Baby.

Prologue
Cason Martin

Cason Martin had perfect feet.

The arches in her feet were high and curved. Inside the pointe shoes were callouses that were thick and hard-earned from the perfection she demanded of just two simple feet.

Right now her perfect feet were throbbing. She felt a new blister crack and bleed as she landed beautifully from her final *jeté*.

"Run it again."

Her deodorant had given up hours ago; her black leotard and ballerina-pink tights now clung to her body in the most uncomfortable and unattractive ways. The energy drink and pain reliever she had for dinner were doing nothing.

"Your fingers look like claws." Natalie huffed around her, correcting the lines of her body, straightening her posture, and adjusting her fingers so that each one was on a different plane. "Soft hands."

Cason didn't say anything; she just flinched as her

body was contorted. With each breath she took, fire circulated through her. Instead of counting beats, Cason counted the thump of blood as it passed through her knee. She stole a look at the leg holding her up in an arabesque and winced.

Her whole thigh was swollen.

It's just a strain.

"Again." Without waiting for a reply, Natalie started the music. Cason began to dance. Heat blasted up her leg as she pushed and strained. The sparks moved in hard, fast pulses to the igniting beat of Stravinsky. With each turn, each small movement, it spread through muscles and tendons. Cason was able to defy gravity with each leap.

"You might do." Natalie released a heavy breath and turned off the speakers. "I don't want you to embarrass the company tomorrow."

"I was the youngest member of your *corps* when I was thirteen, Mom." Irritation moved over Cason like the burning in her knee and thigh.

"And yet, you're still not my best ballerina." No compassion, instead a reminder of how she wasn't living up to her potential. "Run the end combination at home. Soak your feet. Find some facial expressions, you look lifeless."

Cason walked out of the rehearsal, frustration and pain battling with each other. She pulled her coat tighter around her, warding off the cold.

Stars were invisible in the city most nights. The

moonlight was often overshadowed by the street lights and tall buildings. The rehearsal space for the Atlanta Ballet Conservatory was housed in a former cotton mill on the west side of town. The brick was crumbling in parts, but it only added to the old Southern charm.

"Natalie just wants you to be the best." Her mom's assistant patted her on the shoulder. "Did you have Doc Anthony look at your leg?"

"Yeah, just a strain." Cason lied with a smile on her lips. She would most definitely have Doc look at it after her audition tomorrow.

"It's looking a little swollen around your knee. Maybe ice it tonight." With that, Emma got into her car, leaving Cason beside her own.

Sitting on the cold leather seat, the moonlight filtering through the windshield, Cason gently prodded the swelling just above her knee.

It's just a strain.

~

"How's your leg?" Natalie pushed down on Cason's leg as she stretched at the *barre.* They were back at the Atlanta Ballet Conservatory less than ten hours later. Her audition was in an hour. The adjudicators from the American Ballet Theatre were already in another studio, setting up.

"Fine," she said with a tight smile on her face, cutting off the conversation.

"Stretch deeper." Natalie forced Cason's center closer to the floor. Her thigh was burning, muscles pulling, little bubbles that pulsed with pain clawing under her skin and through the fibers of her connective tissue.

"The American Ballet Theatre is running this audition at ABC because of me." It was the start of a very familiar lecture. The underlying message was quite simple: *Do Not Embarrass Me.* "I expect more than your best."

When did Natalie Martin not expect more than Cason's best?

"You only made it in the summer program last year," Natalie reminded her. "You could have spent the last year training under some of the best."

"I know, Mom." Cason counted each popping cell in her thigh muscle. This wasn't pain, this was minor discomfort. This was nothing.

And Cason was just as desperate to get into the Studio Company as her mother was. If she got in, she would move to New York. She would spend her days dancing and dancing and dancing, surrounded by people who understood the release of landing the perfect *grand jeté.*

"Think about it, Cason." Natalie's excitement grew as she pushed Cason's legs farther, taking the stretch deeper, opening her hips. There were at least one hundred reasons Cason wanted to be invited to join the Studio Company of the American Ballet Theatre.

But number one was being away from Natalie Martin.

She stretched, moved, and marked her solo as she waited. The auditions were running on time and only a couple dancers would go before her.

She would dance and leave. There would be no call-backs. Cuts had been made that morning in the company class. Last year during this same audition, Cason had been unable to stop the nerves that had filled her veins, running over her heart, little electric pulses making her normally graceful movements jerky. She had barely made it through the group audition and into the solos.

This year, while the other girls waited, she watched. Watched the way the girls showed off their flexibility, the hyperextension of their knees and hips. The beautiful lifts to their *arabesques.*

Cason bit her lip, refusing to acknowledge the pain in her leg. So much worse than the tiny shocks of nerves, doing so much more damage to her body. Pain had to have an audience to be felt, so she ignored it, pretending that the ache in her muscles was from use, not from injury.

She would be the best.

She was the best.

Being one of Natalie Martin's *prima ballerinas* meant she had to be the best.

The hallway was filled with other dancers, all of them in their leotards and skirts. Some chatted. Cason did not. She closed her eyes and focused on everything but the pain that slid around her tendons and bone, little burning points that tried to pull her attention away from the task at hand.

It's just a strain.

"Cason Martin?" There were routine introductions and reminders of how she would find out if she was being asked to join the company or the summer program. She smiled and nodded, not wanting to appear overly confident.

But she knew.

She knew this audition would get her out of Atlanta and away from the expectations of Natalie Martin.

She gave the assistant her music and made her way to the middle of the floor.

"Whenever you're ready."

She'd started to go up on her toes when she heard the door open and Natalie Martin slipped in. Cason held in her groan of frustration.

There was no smile of pride on Natalie's face, just the tight lips of someone judging every move that she made.

Painful fire fought with the anxiety that slid around her stomach and spine.

Cason let her eyes close for a second.

Focus.

Feel.

Cason pulled in a breath, tightening each muscle in her body. The music was her partner, guiding her as she flew into the air, her *jeté* high and perfect.

Pain chased her, refusing to be ignored, demanding

that she feel each throb. It started right above her knee and exploded up into the muscles in her thigh. Bubbles of heat pulsed through the tendons around her hip. She spun on her toe in a perfect *pirouette* and heat radiated with each twist of her leg. More burning, blinding in a way she hadn't thought possible. She kept dancing. She would move through the flame.

It's just a strain.

Only six counts until it was over. *You can make it.*

One. *Sauté.*

Two. *Piqué.*

Three. *Tendu effacé.*

Her arms stretched beautifully overhead, her right leg supporting her entire body, but her left leg was limp, refusing to point her toe. The crack and Cason's gasp were covered by the ending crescendo of her music.

She held her final pose.

Only the tears on her cheeks gave away her pain.

Cason felt every breath, every heartbeat, every beat of music move through her body as the blaze consumed her entire leg.

It's not a strain.

Prologue
Davis Channing

Davis Channing sat on his hands to keep himself from pulling at the starched collar of his dress shirt. He looked over his shoulder to where his parents were sitting. His mom offered a kind smile with worry on her face, something he had permanently marred her with. Then there was his dad, stoic, but also sitting on his hands. Like Davis. Keeping his fidgets of worry still.

And next to them was Dr. Henderson, the oncologist that had helped save Davis's life just four years ago. He had gray hair and thick eyebrows that sometimes brushed against his glasses. He gave Davis a smile and a small nod of encouragement.

"Mr. Channing." The judge called from her bench. The white collar over her robe was in stark contrast to the robe and her dark skin. The room smelled vaguely of urine and sweat, which Davis would forever associate with the smell of desperation.

"Yes, Your Honor?" Davis now stood; his hands itched to grip the railing in front of him, to find purchase in something that would ground him to this world. Instead, they stayed at his side, flat against his legs, giving off the appearance of being calm.

"I see here you completed an inpatient stay at a rehabilitation facility." She flipped through the report that had been provided by his psychiatrist and counselors at the inpatient rehab Davis had called home for six weeks. "You did well there." She stared at him over her glasses. "Are you continuing treatment now that you've been discharged?"

"Yes, Your Honor. I attend Narcotics Anonymous meetings a few times a week." He wanted to stop his heart from pounding in his chest. "I still see my therapist a couple times a month, and I meet with my NA sponsor frequently." The fact that his NA sponsor was at his school made that easier.

"Your attorney has petitioned the court that your stay in rehab be counted as time served." She flipped through some more paperwork. "Given your health history and your exemplary record since your arrest back in the summer, I'm inclined to agree."

For the first time since Davis Channing was arrested for possession of a controlled substance with intent to distribute, he breathed. It shuttered and stuttered out his chest, pulling his soul out with the breath.

"But—"

Oh no. No. No. No. No. Shit. No.

There was a feeling of lightheadedness, some spots in

front of his eyes. He pushed his fingers into the sides of his thighs, needing a purchase of something. Absently, he realized the rushing in his head was his own breath. Swallowing against the dryness in his mouth, his throat, he fought to control his breath.

"I cannot, in good conscience, let this charge go without there being some restitution." She looked up at Davis, and he saw no compassion, but maybe understanding? His stomach cramped, but he kept his hands at his sides, waiting for whatever the judge had to say. "You are sentenced to 300 hours of community service."

Oh. Davis felt a cold sweat pebble over his skin. He guessed wearing a bright reflective vest and picking up trash couldn't do any more damage to his already dismantled reputation. And thank God it wasn't more time in a cell.

"I have spoken with Dr. Henderson at Children's Hospital, you will report to the oncology clinic there on Monday."

"Excuse me?" Shock pushed down his spine, heat coated his stomach, and now his hands shook.

"Dr. Henderson has asked that you complete the 300 hours of community service at the oncology unit where you were treated. He has stated he thinks it will be good for you to be reminded of what you have been through." The judge looked past him to Dr. Henderson. Davis turned as well, seeing his doctor and parents. They all seemed relieved.

He did not feel relieved.

Davis closed his eyes, not looking at his parents, their fancy attorney, or even the judge behind the bench.

He was going back to the clinic.

He was going to have to go back to the clinic and work.

And see his doctor and his nurses, people he respected. People who loved him.

People he had let down.

Davis began to think more time in a cell wouldn't be so bad after all.

chapter one

Davis spent his lunch hour hiding in the library, college brochures spread out in front of him. A small stack of stickie notes helped him mark where the closest NA meetings were to the various campuses. He had another year of high school after this one, but his latest mantra was all about preparedness.

Plus it gave him something to do. Something so he didn't have to think. Because if he let himself think, he would start thinking about the fact that Cason Martin's name had been on the schedule for the clinic that day.

Oh, this campus has a meeting on-site. He wasn't going to think about Cason Martin, a girl he wasn't sure he could pick out of a line-up, but a name he knew nonetheless. He could think about NA meetings and staying sober.

A distant cacophony pulled him from his thoughts of college NA meetings and not thinking about Cason Martin. Alexis Foster came into the library like a bull. She hurtled through the bookshelves, elbows rocking displays, her entire body crashing into tables and study carrels. Davis hid in the school's library at lunch for just this reason.

Alexis demanded attention.

"Hey there, Davis." Her body leaned on the round table separating them, her arms stretching out to reach him. "You're looking good." She looked at him through makeup-caked lashes.

"What's up, Alexis?" He tried to keep his voice down, not wanting to draw attention to them. Really, he wanted her to leave. And more importantly, leave him alone.

"A date." Her speech was only somewhat slurred. "There's a thing tonight."

"I'm pretty busy here." He motioned to the books and college packets spread in front of him. It was nearly April and Davis had a lot of catching up to do on college visits and essays.

"You know these things don't start until late." She didn't recognize a blow-off when it happened. "You've always been my favorite." Alexis started to reach for him, but Davis moved back before she could.

Davis ran a hand through his short brown hair; he sometimes wished he still wore it long so he could pull it. "I was never your favorite. I brought good dope."

"I bet you could still get good dope." He smelled the chemicals that clung to her. He'd bet she hadn't showered in a week.

"No thanks."

"Come on, I hear that Ethan has got a ton of new shit."

"Alexis, I'm not into that anymore." He stood then, trying to get her away from the prying ears of everyone in the quiet library. Alexis moved in, reaching for anything she could touch on him.

"I need you," she whined, tugging on his shirt sleeve and moving in closer to him. Davis could see the depths of her addiction then, bloodshot eyes, exhaustion, but also being so wired she almost vibrated.

He shouldn't talk to her. He should pull away and find another place to hide, but Davis let her pull him, taking him out of the library and into an empty classroom.

"I know, I screwed up. Okay? I owe Ethan a lot of money."

"I can't help you." He moved away from her quickly, putting empty desks between them. "I don't do that type of thing anymore."

"You can help me!" she begged. "You can get drugs from that hospital."

"No, I can't." The idea alone was stupid. "Alexis, I can't just open up the drug locker and get stuff."

Like a balloon that had a slow leak, Alexis began to dissolve in front of him. "Davis, why did you do it?" Sadness etched into her tired eyes.

"Do what?"

"You left me."

"I was arrested."

"I'm sorry about all of that." She was whining, moving toward irritation in nanoseconds. "I shouldn't have told the cops that you had the dope." When he turned away from her, she only got louder, rage replacing the sorrow from just seconds before. "Your rich parents and fancy lawyer got you out of it anyway."

"Shut up, Alexis." And there was the truth. He knew she didn't want him to come to the party tonight; she wanted his parents' money to come to the party.

"You got a slap on the wrist," she said. "Now your life is a movie of the week with the happy ending and everything. He's going to kill me, Davis." Tears came fast and furious, leaving dark streaks of makeup under her sunken eyes.

"Tell your parents." He softened, his desire to try and help her coming through.

"They kicked me out." Her words stopped him. Alexis had been to countless psychiatrists and programs, but still managed to find a way to use. Never ready to give up the lifestyle. "I've been living with people."

"I'm sorry you were kicked out." There would be no helping Alexis Foster. She had to be the one to decide to be sober.

"You've got to help me, Davis!" Manipulation poured out of her. She tried anything she thought would get him to help her. "This is all your fault!"

"This is not my fault." Anger flared over his words. "I can't fix this for you."

"You got me hooked." Even in withdrawal, she knew exactly where to hit for maximum punch.

"I didn't make you use."

"I used because I wanted you to like me and now I can't

quit." There was a truth there that Davis didn't want to think about. He knew that when he'd first offered to show her how to crush up the prescription pain pill, how to get the best high, that she'd been doing it because of him.

"You don't want to quit." His shoulders sagged in defeat.

"How would you know?" She was yelling. He knew any minute a teacher would return or someone would hear her.

"You can get help."

"Oh yeah, what should I do?"

"There are ways to get help, protection, people who want to help you."

"Maybe I'll just tell Ethan that you've got my money." Davis ignored the stupid threat.

Ethan wouldn't come after Davis.

Right?

"You can get help." He tried once more, wishing he could find the girl he'd known before. Before scoring had become their only desires.

"Fuck that, Davis." She spit. Her personality switched again, anger lacing her words, her posture. "I just need money to get him off my back."

"I know."

"I only ever liked you for your money, you know."

"I know, Alexis."

If you go, you could get high. The words tickled his brain, down his spine, over his extremities. And instantly, he could taste the high. Feel it pulling on his stomach and speeding up his heart. God, it would be so easy.

"Just give me the fuckin' money." She started toward him, rage pulsing from every pore of her exhausted and used body. "I can make your life hard, Davis."

"Is there a problem here, Ms. Foster?" One of the teachers on hall duty found them, and Davis had never been more grateful for them.

"No, Mrs. Lewis." Alexis sounded like the model student. Not an addict begging him for money.

"Mr. Channing?"

"I'm fine." He shoved his hands in his pockets, feelings of hate began to stir in his gut. Alexis was garnering him unwanted attention from teachers, he knew that Mrs. Lewis was going to think he was using again. *Damnit.* "I was just leaving to go see Mr. Williams."

"Ms. Foster, you're coming with me."

"The hell I am." Alexis screamed. Davis left. He didn't need to watch her come apart right in front of him.

He ran from the room and straight to Mr. Williams in the guidance counselor's office.

"Davis?"

Mr. Williams was one of the four guidance counselors at his school, and by a stroke of luck (or the crappy karma he deserved), he was also Davis's sponsor through the NA program.

"Mr. Williams." A perpetual hippie in a modern society. When Davis had first started meeting with him, he'd thought that he was a complete poser, but the more he met with him, the more he realized he was just forgetful about the minute details of day-to-day life. Mr. Williams also frequently forgot to wear socks.

"What's up?"

"Alexis hit me up for money and dope." There was no way to ease into this conversation. No starting with small talk or a general check-in. "And it pisses me off so much that it almost makes me want to use again."

"Funny how that happens." Mr. Williams didn't have wizened eyes or brows that arched with question. He looked sort of tired, eyes dropping at the sides, and he constantly pinched the bridge of his nose.

"It's such trash." Davis pushed at his temples with his fingers, trying to burrow into his brain, maybe scrape out the part of his mind that demanded a release only found in a high. "I don't want to use. I don't want to be that guy again, but it feels like it would just be so much easier."

"Probably not, though." Mr. Williams gulped at his coffee. Davis knew from the time he spent with him that it was either black or loaded with so much cream and sugar that you couldn't taste the coffee. Nothing in between. "How many days sober are you, Davis?"

"229. I'm still going to at least one meeting a week."

"How is it going?" Mr. Williams's lips thinned, pressed into a line.

This was a tricky question. He didn't miss the high nor the drugs. He missed the ease of his life back then, when his only struggle was getting his next high, not constantly convincing himself that he enjoyed being sober. "There are good days and bad. I miss the drugs like I miss having cancer. So, in other words, not at all."

"Remember that your journey is not over. Addiction is a disease, and like your cancer, it's something you have to keep a check on and keep working at."

"Yeah. I don't plan on using again." And he didn't, but that didn't mean the sharp desire didn't often fill him in painful ways.

"I wouldn't be truthful if I didn't remind you that relapse and struggles are symptoms of your disease. Not failures, just part of it. I'm not saying you will relapse or that you will always want to use, but it's just part of it."

"I hate to think of it." Trying to digest the reminder made Davis feel like he had swallowed a brick whole. The sharp edges and rough sides were sitting in his throat and he was painfully working them down into his stomach, where the brick would sit until his insides finally gave up.

Mr. Williams pushed his readers down and peered at Davis over them. "Your teachers are pretty impressed with what you've been turning in lately."

"I do want to go to college." Davis pulled at the thread in his jeans.

"Your probation is about up."

"Yeah, I've got a couple weeks left on my community service." Davis looked up at him and then back down at the floor. "Do you think the hospital would let me continue to stay on after my hours are filled?"

"You mean as a volunteer?"

"Yeah."

"Dr. Henderson has said that you've been really great around the oncology clinic lately."

"I talked to him about it last week." Davis studied his knee intently, looking for words that never seemed right. "I think it'd look good on my college transcripts." Davis glanced up, almost afraid to see Mr. Williams's reaction. "My grades from last year aren't as good as they could have been, and volunteer hours might help a little."

"The community service we set up wasn't the epic fail you first said it would be, huh?"

"It turned out okay. Dr. Henderson isn't quite the tool I said he was."

"If I remember, you had another, not quite as tactful name for your oncologist."

"I didn't want him to give me grief about how he worked really hard to save my life and then I was ruining all his work."

"Did you come up with that all on your own?" Mr. Williams laughed.

"Are you kidding? He *still* reminds me how I almost destroyed myself, and I've been clean for seven months."

"Remember why you got sober." Mr. Williams spoke softly, his thin, lined face growing serious. "Remember what sobriety means to you."

"Life." Davis laughed a little desperately. "Staying sober means I get to live my life."

"What's something else?" Mr. Williams prodded. "Something tangible."

"Seeing my parents start to trust me again."

"That's true. But, what's something that's just for you?"

Davis sat in the fake leather chair and thought about his counselor's question. What was something that Davis got back for being sober? Yeah, being healthy and living were great things. He liked the fact that his mom no longer had that constant worry line between her eyes. Without thought, his fingers found a small, round coin in his hoodies pocket. It had the words "Be Brave" etched into it, a reminder.

"Camp," he finally said. "I can go back to Camp Chemo if I'm clean."

"I've heard you talk about camp." Mr. Williams leaned back, his loafer flipping off the bottom of his foot. "It's just for kids who have cancer."

"Or had it." Davis loved Camp Chemo. "I want to go back to camp."

"Then remember that when it gets hard." Mr. Williams scratched the back of his head. "It's not something that just goes away."

"Right." Davis nodded, not saying more because he could still taste it. Like a phantom pain for a limb that was gone, the high pulled at him.

chapter Two

Starting chemotherapy on April Fools' Day was the worst kind of joke.

This was her life now: sitting in different waiting rooms. Meeting countless nurses and doctors. Someone was always taking her blood, or taking an x-ray, or taking her vitals. Cason had been giving to so many people, she was turning into a hollowed-out husk of whom she used to be.

Just a few weeks ago, she'd sat in this very same clinic, in this very same chair, and felt her entire world slide to the left. Sure, it was still her life, but everything had changed to the point that it was like she'd fallen through a wormhole or time warp. Everything still looked the same, the world was still spinning, but her entire life was forever changed.

Dr. Henderson had looked at Cason and as delicately as he could, had destroyed her life. "I'm sorry, Cason, but you have an aggressive, cancerous tumor on your knee." In that one moment, her perfect, prima-ballerina, pink-tutu world fell off its pointe.

She wasn't Cason Martin, prima ballerina, anymore. She was Cason Martin, number T7654908, cancer patient.

She had sat in one of the childish exam rooms. Everything was in bright primary colors; hell, even the ceiling tiles had been painted. Dr. Henderson had these bushy eyebrows that made Cason want to take some wax or something to them and try to make them point up, like a villain in an old silent movie. She should have been focused on what the doctor was saying. It was probably life and death news, but she could only hear ocean waves and could only stare at his overly ambitious brows.

She looked at him, trying to focus, as he told her that the pain and fatigue she'd been dealing with was not because of stress and a dance injury.

Instead, when her leg had given out on her during the audition, her femur had crumbled into tiny pieces. And the strongest bone in her body had crumbled because it was obliterated by a tumor that was growing and eating her bones. Until that moment, she hadn't really believed that kids got cancer. She'd always thought it was a plot device.

Now today, Monday, was the first day of her very first chemotherapy session.

How could this be her life? She was missing countless rehearsals and classes. Not to mention her school work. She might have only attended school for half a day, but if she wanted to graduate, she was going to have keep to up.

Anxiety filled her gut, tingling and skirting around her abdomen before chasing signals and making its way up her nervous system, attaching itself to all her nerve endings. She took a deep breath, refusing to let it get the better of her. She would stay calm. She would not scream and cry like her soul begged her to do.

The unforgiving hospital chair beneath her was hard, her braced leg sticking straight out, her knee unmovable. It was uncomfortable at best, bordering on painful. She tried to shift her weight, but it only caused the brace to dig into her skin.

"Let me help." A dark-haired boy around her age came over, taking a chair and sliding it under her leg. She vaguely recognized him but couldn't quite place him. "Any better?"

"It helps." The shift took the pressure off her leg, relieving the stress that pulled on her back. "Thanks."

He was cute, she'd give him that. His dark eyes were fringed with thick, long lashes that she could only get with those horrid fake ones. He sat down next to her, pulling posters across his lap. "You new?"

"What gave me away?" She pulled at the fraying Velcro on the top strap of her brace.

"Your hair's not a wig. And the brace." He smiled knowingly, like he'd seen all of this before.

"Oh." She didn't want to talk about her cancer, starting chemotherapy, or any of those realities. She wanted to pretend she was at this clinic for any other reason. She didn't want to give him anything.

"Davis Channing, I think we go to school together."

His eyes crinkled at the sides; his off-center smile lifted. She would have to be comatose not to notice just how attractive that smile was. "I volunteer here." He extended his hand.

"Davis!" she smiled. "Of course." Then it all clicked. "I thought you were in rehab," she blurted. Heat rushed up her chest, neck, and into her cheeks.

"Not anymore." The laugh lines smoothed out, showing no embarrassment, just kindness. "I was a cancer kid first."

"Oh my God," she exhaled. "That's right." Brushing her hair out of her eyes, she looked up at him. "I guess I get to join your club." The words were slow; she was hearing them for the first time as she spoke, telling another person she had cancer.

Davis scanned the room. "Where's your mom?"

"Talking to someone about a bill." She motioned over to the windowed desk where her mother was. "Something about our insurance coverage."

"You'll be surprised how much you learn about the healthcare system during this." He drummed his fingers over the posters, bringing her attention back to them. She could almost make out a few kids, but that was it. The clinic was noisy, a mix of bright colors and relaxing tones. Magazines and books littered small, round end tables. Arcade games and toddler TV played in a corner.

Standing up, he said, "I've got to get back to work,

but text me if you need anything." He took her phone and put his number in. "I'm here all the time."

"Why?" She wrinkled her nose. "I would think you'd have had enough of this place."

"Community service."

He said it so honestly, so openly that it stopped her. She didn't know how to process that.

"Thanks again." She motioned to the chair. Davis walked down the hall, hanging the posters.

"Who was that?" Natalie sat down, shoving a bill into her purse and taking out her iPad all in one smooth motion.

"Davis Channing, we go to school together."

Natalie's eyes narrowed, watching Davis as he worked. "Channing, as in Amanda Channing's son?"

"We haven't really gotten past basics." Cason could just see the posters. Kids in a pool, some bald, most who looked somewhat healthy. Fascinating.

She was called back to the treatment area, and the nurses accessed her port, Cason's newest "accessory" that was implanted when they had done the biopsy to assess her tumor. When the nurse pushed the fluid to flush the line, the taste of the saline filled her mouth, making her gag. She knew with chemo starting later that morning that it was only going to get worse.

There was a knock, followed by the entrance of Cason's new oncologist. "Dr. Henderson." Natalie smiled like the savior of the world had walked into the room.

Cason's reaction to the man who had told her she had cancer was the opposite. Her heart thudded deeply in her chest, nearly stopping; she could feel her blood thicken and pool in the deepest parts of her stomach. Realistically, she knew he wasn't responsible. Her leg, the fire that had burned in it at the audition, was diseased long before he said the words, but it was like her brain couldn't help but hate him.

"Good morning, Cason, Natalie." He always greeted her first. She would have preferred he forget she existed. Maybe if he only talked to her mom about all of this, then it wouldn't be real. She wouldn't be sick. She wouldn't have cancer. Instead, she'd be restless with anxiety over finding out if she was accepted into ABT's Studio Company.

"Today is the big day!" Natalie said it like Cason was starting college, not like she was about to be pumped full of toxins and poisons. She'd read about the side effects of these drugs. They'd kill her just as quickly as cancer could.

Cason was brought back to reality when Dr. Henderson moved closer and began an exam, listening to her heart and lungs. It was like every exam she'd ever gotten from her pediatrician before she'd started seeing the doctor who treated the dancers at the Atlanta Ballet Conservatory.

"The chemo will be rough, but we'll find a combination of anti-nausea meds to help."

"Cason is a dancer," Natalie interjected. "She's used to tough."

Cason thought that was the most idiotic thing she'd heard lately. Cancer and dancing had absolutely nothing in common and could never be compared on the scale of toughness.

It was obvious that Natalie Martin was not the one with a disease or she would know this.

chapter Three

Davis collected toys as he moved around the nurses' station. Spots glared behind his eyes, mimicking the pain there. He tried to ignore them, hoping they would disappear. Headaches were an everyday occurrence since he'd become sober.

He listened to the sounds of nurses and techs taking care of the patients. Every Monday and Friday, he was obligated to be at the oncology clinic at the children's hospital. He liked coming to the clinic, hanging out with patients who, in small ways, needed him. He'd had no idea how much he'd enjoy being helpful.

His job was to clean the toys and get out of the way. If a patient needed him, Heather, the Child Life Specialist, would find him, but right now most of the patients were occupied. Four years ago, it had been his family at the clinic, and Davis had been starting his own chemotherapy treatments for non-Hodgkin's lymphoma.

He hurriedly finished putting the playroom back together and went to rest in the staff/volunteer lounge. Seeing Cason Martin in the waiting room had shocked him. Even though he knew she was going to be there, it was out of context. But there she was, pretty Cason Martin with her long, blond hair and blue eyes that seemed both terrified and exhausted.

He hadn't wanted to tell her that it was all going to get worse before it ever got any better. Pinching the bridge of his nose, Davis let his head roll back against the couch and closed his eyes. He could still see the way that Cason's mom had looked at him, following him as he hung up the posters around the clinic.

Would he ever be able to forget that he was an addict?

No. The word was whispered into his brain, circling through the gray matter and then sliding into his heart.

"Davis." Dr. Henderson walked in. "Hungover?" Davis wasn't sure whether to tell him to stop yelling or to reassure him he was fine.

"A hangover would be welcome at this point." He sat up. "Just a bad headache."

"Sharp or throbbing?" Dr. Henderson sat down and immediately felt along Davis's neck, checking his lymph nodes. One of the major drawbacks of doing your community service with your oncologist was the personal attention. Dr. Henderson didn't ask, he just did, when it came to Davis's health.

"Uh, both?"

"Probably a sinus headache, but if it doesn't go away by the end of your shift, let me know and I'll get you some stronger sinus stuff." *Stuff* was a medical term in Dr. Henderson's world. "How's it going?"

His unreliable brain searched for words. "Odd."

There was something about Dr. Henderson that made Davis a fountain of information.

"Explain." Dr. H got a soda from the fridge. As far as Davis knew, that was his only vice.

"I ran into Alexis recently."

"Alexis from your days of smoking dope?"

"Yes."

"When you nearly destroyed something I worked tirelessly to cure?" There was humor in his voice, but Davis also knew there was truth. Dr. H cared about all his patients. He didn't want them to just survive their cancer, but to live full lives.

"That's right. Thanks for the reminder."

"It's what I'm here for." Dr. H waited for Davis to continue. He had no problem with a lingering silence.

Davis told the story of Alexis barging into the library. She had been strung out and lonely, barely a shadow of whom she used to be. It bothered Davis. He remembered the once-vibrant girl that she had been, and he felt responsible for who she was now.

"I want to help her. I want to do something," Davis said with a trace of bitterness, "but I can't. Alexis is on her own. No one can rescue you from addiction."

"Glad to see those meetings are working out for you." Dr. H glanced down as his phone buzzed. "Ah, I must return to work."

"I don't think you ever stop working."

"My wife would agree." He stopped at the door. "Davis, I'm really happy to see the progress you've made."

They both left the break room, making their way down the hall. "I'm not going to let Alexis trip me up again," Davis said.

"Good." Dr. Henderson turned into an exam room. Checking his watch, Davis realized he had just enough time to grab a soda from the vending machine before he needed to start the craft project in the treatment room.

The cafeteria of the hospital was always busy, it didn't matter what time of day it was. There were always residents, who looked more tired than anyone had the right to look, trying to get a quick bite. Parents and patients, siblings, anyone who just needed to get out of their rooms. Even his own mom, it seemed.

"Mom," Davis called through the busy hallway. She was coming out of one of the meeting rooms.

"Hi, sweetie." His mom pulled him into a hug and kissed his cheek. He welcomed the affection, grateful for it.

Amanda Channing was as close to perfect as a mom could be. She'd been his den mother for Cub Scouts, his T-ball coach, and "momcologist" when he'd been diagnosed. Davis couldn't remember a time in his life when his mother wasn't actively present in what was going on with him. Even when he'd done everything he could to get her to go away.

"I heard about Cason Martin." She walked with him toward the vending machines.

"How?" Davis shouldn't have been surprised. His

mother always knew. She fed the machine a couple bills and punched the button for his customary soda.

"I ran into Betsy, Paige's mom, at the hospital parent support group. She said there was a new girl who was a dancer on the floor." His mom helped often with the parent support group, trying to show the parents that there would be life after cancer. "I put it together after that."

"All anyone knows about Cason is that she's a dancer." He pulled at a loose thread on the hem of his shirt until his mom swatted his hand to make him stop. "She has bone cancer." The rest of the sentence didn't need to be said.

"Remember it's out of our control." Amanda ruffled his hair like he was twelve. "It's out of everyone's control, but we can pray. We can send out good thoughts." He hated those words. It never felt active enough for him. He wanted to be able to do something.

"You should give her mom info on the parent support group when you go back to the clinic." She handed him her card and a flier on the support group.

"How did you know she had chemo today?"

"I know all," his mom laughed. "Natalie is going to need some help. If you see her, let her know I'm happy to talk or bring dinner by." She kissed his cheek once more and they split, his mom going back to her car and Davis making his way to the clinic. He held his mom's card and the flier.

It gave him a great reason to stop and see Cason.

chapter Four

Sleep was a relief.

While Cason was sleeping, she was only vaguely un-comfortable. When the chemo had started to drip, she hadn't felt anything. For the first hour or so, she had flipped through her magazines, her books, she'd listened to various playlists, and even watched a little daytime television. Then, slowly, it had hit her, starting out as annoying then working its way to full-out sickness.

There was a knock, but unlike the medical profes-sionals, the person on the other side actually waited for her to answer. "Come in." God, she sounded like she had gargled rocks.

Davis had barely gotten into the room before she was retching into the blue emesis bag. Cason spit, ridding her mouth of the bile that coated her throat and tongue. "Sorry." She gagged over the words.

"It's okay." Davis appeared completely unfazed by her throwing up. "I saw your mom leave and thought you might need company." He handed her a wet hand towel to put around her neck.

"She's at lunch." She heaved. "She didn't want the smell to make me sick."

"Poor timing."

"Throwing up is gross." Cason's breath trembled out as she fought to hold onto her composure. "I hate it."

"No one likes it," Davis assured her. "But most everyone does it."

"I guess I couldn't be unique this time." She gave a weary sigh and closed her eyes. Shades of green and blue danced under her lids as she tried to imagine *pas de deux* and *grand jetés*. Instead, all she could see was the swirling color of stomach bile.

"I'm back." Natalie was unhappy. Cason was too sick, too tired, too everything to care that her mother was irritated at the one person who stuck around to help.

"I'm Davis Channing," she heard Davis stand and answer. Her eyes opened just enough to watch her mother start to turn an interesting shade of violet.

Natalie didn't smile. "I remember when you were diagnosed."

"I volunteer on the oncology floor a few days a week now." Davis then turned his full, crooked smile at her mother.

"Why?" Her mother had no pleasantries for him. "It's depressing." She was standing ramrod straight, the same posture she used with dancers who pissed her off. Natalie Martin was attempting to intimidate Davis.

"I got sentenced to some community service and this is where I ended up." He shrugged and the look of absolute contriteness on his face was the first thing in hours to make Cason smile. "I wanted to leave some information about Camp Chemo and the parent support group for you guys." He motioned to something on the counter next to the sink.

Natalie Martin had barely blinked when Cason was diagnosed with a deadly bone tumor, but the idea of attending a support group made her visibly recoil. If she gritted her teeth any harder, she was going to need dentures, the muscle in her jaw ticking in rapid fire. "Thank you." She said it so tightly that Cason thought she might start shooting lasers at any minute.

"My mom said she'd love to talk to you if you want." Davis didn't appear to care that Natalie wanted him gone. He shifted his feet in that relaxed way that said he was going to stay a while. "She mentioned something about bringing dinner by."

"We are fine." Natalie had no chill. "If you don't mind . . ."

"Cason, let me know if you need anything from school. I'm happy to grab it for you." Davis smiled again. She wasn't sure if it was to piss off her mother or to try and win her over. "You need a support system during this. That's one of the great things about Camp Chemo. Everyone there gets it."

"We are fine." Natalie practically spit the words. She crossed the room and opened the door for him.

"Thanks, Davis." Cason tried to soften the tension her mother was flinging at him. "I appreciate it."

"Anytime. I was serious earlier, text if you need something." He stepped back, taking his time exiting the room.

"I will." She didn't realize she was smiling at him until she saw Natalie's face.

"I'll see you around." He smiled for Cason alone, and right then, he went from cute to devastatingly hot, leaving Natalie fuming and Cason feeling just a little better.

"He's nice." Cason laid back on the bed, closing her eyes, but even closed, she could feel her mom getting more irritated by the moment. She could hear the *click-click-click* of Natalie's heels on the linoleum floor, could feel the anger pouring off her.

"He's a delinquent," Natalie said, her heels stopping shortly. "I remember hearing he was arrested for drugs or something."

"I thought you were above gossip."

"It's not gossip if it's true."

Cason peeked an eye open to see her mom throwing the brochures Davis had brought into the trash. "We do not need some ridiculous camp or support group." Natalie sat in the recliner in a huff. "This is just a stupid inconvenience and it will all be over soon. We will be moving on with our lives."

While part of Cason agreed, she was already completely over chemotherapy and it was only her first day. She did think that it was a little nice to have someone who didn't gag when she vomited.

"You don't need some depressing camp." Natalie was on a tear. "Who would want to sit in the woods and talk about all of this?" This was said with such derision that Cason felt like she should apologize. "You will be back at the *barre* by Christmas. Just eight months."

"Right." But even as she said the word, she knew it was a lie.

chapter Five

Davis stood at the counter of the Daily Grind. He was waiting for Mark, a regular, to order his coffee. Davis knew that Mark had been laid off from his temp job the week before. He'd overheard as Mark had all but begged for a little more time to get money before his lights got shut off.

"Hey, man," Davis held up a cup of his regular coffee and a bagel sandwich. "I made this for lunch, but forgot that I had plans. Want it?" He could easily fix himself something to eat later.

"I'm just a little short this week," Mark started to refuse.

"I'm just going to throw it out." Davis cut in as he handed him the plate. "It's yours."

Mark studied the food for a minute before looking up at Davis. "Thanks, man."

Without warning, a snake curled in Davis's belly, the smell of chemicals and the taste of the high filled his brain and mouth. A physical ache punched into his stomach, pushing his diaphragm up, making it impossible for him to breathe. It was always like this, no warning and often very little reason why, but he was desperate to get high.

He wanted to use.

He wanted something, anything to take the feelings of frustration and to make them go away. He could feel the pills in his hands, the way the smoke would curl up around his nose, and the anticipation of the high.

Instead, he grabbed his phone.

Davis [3:33PM]: Are you around?
Jase [3:33PM]: Three blocks away.
Davis [3:34PM]: Come to the Grind. Coffee on me.

Davis didn't have to say more. Jase would know.

"Davis?" Jase, one of his oldest camp friends, came into the shop. "You okay?"

"You couldn't have better timing." He let out a strangled laugh.

"Bad day?" Jase's code for "Are you thinking about using?"

"The worst." Davis blew out a breath, exhaling the taste of crushed pills and smoke, willing it to just leave his body. "Talk to me, man." Davis tried to clear his head, but the plea from his brain for just one more hit was a siren's call. "How's Mari?"

"You know my girl. She's already plotting how they're going to win Capture the Flag." Jase sat at the counter. "She is very serious about this."

"As always." Davis blew out a hard breath and got his friend a coffee. "It'll be fun to be back at camp."

"I heard about the new girl from Mari." Jase sipped his coffee.

Davis drummed his fingers over the counter between them. Nervous energy now filled the void that had just been begging for a high. "Cason has Ewing's and I wanted to know what it was. She's a dancer. Like, professional. I wanted to know her chances of dancing again."

"My mom said something about it." Jase's parents were part of the country club set. "Mom's on the Board of Directors of the ballet. She mentioned they had to move the next meeting to a Saturday to accommodate Cason's mom," Jase explained.

"Yeah, Natalie is the director or something." Davis sipped and studied the coffee. No answers were there, despite how much he wanted them to be. "Cason has a bone tumor." His gut tightened. "How does Mari handle having one leg?" Davis didn't know for sure what Cason's surgical options were, but knew that amputation was probably one of them. Maybe if she could talk to his friends . . . An idea began to simmer in the back of his brain.

Jase moved his fingers over his knee in a repeating pattern, working out his own anxiety. "I know she has her moments of doubt, where she wants to be like everyone else and there's nothing she can do about it. She can brush it off, make fun of it, but I see it in her eyes. My family didn't always make it easy either. Cason will experience doubt no matter what the outcome is."

"How could I help a girl who might lose her leg?"

"Aren't you a little invested? Didn't she just start chemo?" Jase attempted to raise one eyebrow, something only Mari could do.

"Probably," Davis laughed, but it didn't convince either of them. "I just get the feeling she doesn't have a lot of friends."

Jase was quiet for a minute, but didn't grill Davis anymore. "I've only ever dated Mari when she's had one leg." Jase moved his fingers in a clicking motion as he thought through his words. "Hell, I've only ever known her with one leg. You can't ignore what's going on. I don't know." He wasn't done speaking, still searching for the right words. "Listen. I think that's the best thing you can do."

"Right." The vibration from Davis's phone jerked him back to reality, pulling his attention. "It's Cason."

Cason [4:01PM]: Are you busy?
Davis [4:02PM]: At work, but I get off in an hour.

"She's texting you? Mari didn't tell me about this." Jase patted his friend on the shoulder, rising. "I've got to run and pick her up from work. Remember, you have to take care of you first. Then you can help her." The unspoken words rang in Davis's head.

Don't use.

Stay clean.

Just one hit. His brain whispered instead.

No one has to know. The words itched and slid around the synapses, shocking his impulses, filling his mouth with a desire so strong it stole his breath. It left him empty and hollow.

And still, lingering in the deepest parts of his brain, it whispered, *Just one.*

chapter six

Day five of her first round of therapy. There had been some good to come out of all of this, and currently he was unabashedly flirting with her from across the room. Her treatments lasted approximately six hours. She would spend the morning sleeping and rise just in time to see Davis arrive at the clinic from school.

Another good thing was watching Natalie turn purple when Davis was around.

Cason sat in one of the recliners. Her room was being used for some kid who had to be sedated. Natalie got comfortable in her own chair, pulling out her laptop to check her email, while Cason put her earbuds in and scanned her homework. Keeping up with school during chemo was no different than when she was out all the time for dance. A perk of being a professional was she only had to take core classes. Missing school wasn't too different for her because she normally only went half a day anyway.

"Good morning!" Heather, the child life specialist, sat down across from them. She was maybe in her thirties and had long, golden hair tied up in a couple of pens. Cason tried to ignore the fact that she was wearing a

T-shirt emblazoned with the logo for Camp Chemo. "Cason, you seem to be doing well today."

"Hi." Natalie was skepticism personified. "I don't believe we've met."

"Oh, sorry! I'm Heather McNeil. I'm here to help you guys in any way you need. Child life specialists work with the docs and nurses to offer things they can't always do. I think you've been at lunch the few times I've been able to drop by."

"I'm feeling okay." Cason didn't know what to think of Heather. She was always going from one patient to another, sometimes meeting individually with patients or helping them through a procedure.

"Need an iPad or a magazine for after your homework. And for you, Mrs. Martin, I help get the support group together."

"We do not need a support group," Natalie was quick to interject. "We're fine."

"Some parents lead it, I just tell folks about it."

"One of your volunteers already told us." Natalie managed to put her iPad away to focus her ire on Heather. "And do you really think it's best practice for the hospital to have a known drug abuser in the hospital?"

"Oh, you've met Davis." Heather smiled, not at all put out by Natalie's harsh words or condemnation. "It was Dr. Henderson's idea. We don't just forget about our patients once they are no longer in treatment. We treat the whole family here. Cancer doesn't just affect the patient. We often work with patients after their therapy, Davis included."

"I would prefer that he have very little contact with my daughter."

"Mom, don't be stupid," Cason finally cut in. She liked Davis. She liked the way he irritated Natalie. "I go to school with him."

"You don't need that kind of exposure."

"Please." She rolled her eyes. "I did go to a public high school."

"Davis is around a lot. He's great with the patients and really helps families out." Heather stood, officially done with Natalie Martin, it seemed. "I'm happy to help you with anything you need, Cason. Please don't hesitate to utilize the Child Life team." She turned to Cason's mother. "The same goes for you, Mrs. Martin. Please let us know how we can help." She left a coloring book, some markers, and a stack of cards. Cason still wasn't sure exactly how she felt about Heather McNeil, but she couldn't be that bad.

~

Lunchtime meant Natalie would run down to the cafeteria for her customary salad and Cason would get a few minutes of peace. She was still in one of the recliners out in the main hub of the treatment room. She'd heard Davis call it the fishbowl because the patients were in the center of the room, able to see all that was going on around them. There were curtains if they needed privacy, but Cason had noticed that most people preferred to leave them open so they could see or chat with neighbors.

"Mom gone?" With Natalie out of the clinic, Heather sat down in her vacated space.

Cason took her ear buds out. "Trying to get things squared away at work. She tells me she's just getting lunch, but I know she's talking to the choreographers and the managers."

"It won't be forever." Heather shuffled a deck of cards, dealing out a hand of Uno for them. "As soon as this becomes more routine, she'll be able to go back to work some."

"Uno?" Cason arched a brow. "Really?"

"It gives you a good break from studying." Heather flipped a card. "It's mindless, there's no real skill, and you can talk while we play."

"Talk?" Cason's brows knitted together, letting Heather know exactly how she felt about talking.

"Tell me about how things with your mom are going."

"She hasn't had to be a mom in a while." Cason played a skip card and then a red seven. "Not that she's bad, Natalie Martin has just been a dance director for a long time." A wisp of a smile crossed Cason's lips as she re-played the words she'd spoke. "I think these drugs take away my filter."

"Probably." Heather played a red eight. "Do you miss dancing?"

Cason didn't answer immediately. She studied her cards the way that a fortune teller studied a crystal ball. But there were no words floating around in a fog or written neatly on her cards that could help her explain how she felt.

"Yes," she stated simply. "Sometimes I feel like I can't breathe." There was an ache in her chest as she thought about it, but it wasn't because of her accessed port.

"What do you mean?" Heather grinned as she played a draw four when Cason only had one card left. "I don't let teenagers win, just the under-ten crowd, and then only on days they need an ego boost."

"I didn't *just* dance. It's who I am." Cason stared at her cards and then looked up quickly. "Who I was." Heather started to say something to give her hope, but right then, Cason couldn't hear it. If she had to listen to another person tell her that she would be dancing again soon, or that it was an opportunity to find other hobbies, she would scream.

"And I've lost all semblance of independence. I can't even shower by myself."

"That is tough," Heather agreed, seeming to see that Cason couldn't talk about dancing more. Not yet anyway. "Play a card. How have your friends taken the news?" Heather played another draw four and Cason scowled.

"I don't have a lot of friends," Cason admitted softly. "I mean, I dance. That's what I do."

"What about the people you dance with?"

"You mean my mother's employees?" Cason smiled. "I am strictly off limits."

"That's Jared." Heather motioned to an African-American boy who was getting a blood transfusion. Davis was with him, and the boy's family was playing a loud and physical game of Slaps. The raucous laughter was loud and energetic, filling the clinic floor and making them both smile. "His favorite person in the world is Davis." Heather's smile softened. "Davis works his schedule so that he can be here when Jared is."

"That's kind." Cason watched the two boys. Davis was all grins and fake-outs as they played full contact. He looked over to them, and directed a slow, overly flirtatious smile at her. Flushing, she looked back at her cards.

"That's Davis in a nutshell." Heather shook her head at their antics. "He's a pain in my ass, but he's got a good heart."

"He's here a lot."

"He's been coming in more to make sure that some of his patients are okay." Cason could hear the unspoken words. She was now one of his patients. "Camp applications will go out soon. They go out about four months before camp, so he'll spend time talking parents into letting their kids go and talking to those kids who think they don't want to go."

"Camp?" She felt like she might have been masterfully played and led to this conversation.

"There's a cancer camp. If you're between seven and

eighteen years old, you can go." Cason watched as Heather shuffled and dealt the cards out again. She was going to talk Dr. Henderson into giving her chemo the week of camp. "It's pretty fun. I go most years."

"Yo! Channing!" The conversation was thankfully cut short by a girl with dark-brown hair and hot-pink crutches. She moved into the treatment room like she owned the place. Her crutches were a graceful extension of her body, not the cage that Cason felt.

"Oh God, I forgot Mari was on the schedule for today." Heather laughed and sighed at the same time. "Hey, princess, this is a hospital where sick kids are. Keep it down."

Davis paused his game with Jared and ran to Mari, wrapping her in a hug that lifted her off the ground, crutches and all.

"Another one of his patients?" Was there a twinge of jealousy in her voice? What did she care?

"No, Mari's a friend from camp."

"Oh, are we talking about camp?" Mari asked as she sat down with Heather and Cason. She pulled herself a hand of the Uno cards and immediately joined the game. "Hi, I'm Mari."

"Cason."

"Ewing's or Osteogenic?" Mari referred to the two most common types of bone tumors.

"Uh, Ewing's." Cason didn't feel like she could catch her breath. Who was this girl?

"The brace gave you away." Mari nodded toward Cason's outstretched leg. "I had osteo." Mari played a card. "You should come to camp this summer."

"I was just telling her," Heather said as she played a reverse, sending it back to Mari. "I was attempting to be a little more low-key about it."

"Why be low-key?" Mari drew a handful of cards. "Camp is seriously great. I like to say it's the only place where hair and limbs are optional."

"Oh." Cason didn't like the sound of this place at all. Or this girl.

"I know you think you don't want to go." Mari smiled and softened, something resembling understanding crossing her face. "But I promise, it's awesome. Like, it's the only place I really feel like I fit in."

"Mari doesn't fit in many places though," said Davis as he sat down with them.

"Har har." Mari faked a laugh. "Cason, how long have you been on treatment?"

"Fifth day." And she was starting to feel exhausted just from this girl's energy. But at least she hadn't puked that day.

"So, no surgical discussions yet." Mari played a card, but Cason barely registered it. "I hated those."

"Why?" Cason heard herself ask, but really she wanted to put her head in the sand. Then she could pretend that she wouldn't have to make this type of decision. Ever since the biopsy, she'd let herself pretend that she wasn't going to need another surgery. That her leg was fine, just a little cancer, something easy to take care of.

"They made me anxious, but I was only ten, so I didn't have the words to say that. I hated knowing my parents felt like they had to make this big and important decision about limb sparing versus amputation or rotationplasty. I felt like I had to keep insisting that I was okay, that it would all be okay."

"It is, right?" Cason spoke softly. "After your amputation?" She hated saying that word. It felt like if she said it, she was somehow saying that it was a possibility for her.

"I had a limb salvage first," Mari stared at her cards, reorganizing them, "but needed an amputation in the end. It wasn't my first choice, but it's why I'm alive."

"Cason, do you know your surgical options?" Heather moved the conversation back to her.

"Just the basics." She didn't want to talk about her choices. Because the words were scary. The words meant this was all real and something that was happening. "I think we're planning on a limb salvage procedure." Cason suddenly wanted to ask a thousand questions, because a nudging inside said Mari would explain the damage control of cutting out cancer in an intrinsic way that Dr. Henderson wasn't capable of.

She wanted to know why Mari wasn't wearing a prosthesis. She wanted to know what it was like. *Were phantom pains a real thing? Why do you use forearm crutches instead of the ones that went under your arms? Did any of this ever get any easier?* But she was quiet. She couldn't figure any of it out.

"Your mom is back," Davis said.

Cason's stomach heaved and it had nothing to do with her chemotherapy. For a few minutes, she had been able to talk about her cancer, to talk about the possibilities without it being wrapped around her career as a dancer. Natalie Martin couldn't talk about her cancer unless she also said ballet in the same sentence.

"We should get everyone together before camp," Mari said, excitement growing in her voice. "Let Cason meet Noah."

"And Jase?" Davis teased.

"My boyfriend." Mari explained to Cason. "He'd get his feelings hurt if we didn't invite him."

"Excuse me," Natalie interrupted the conversation.

"Hi!" Mari smiled but Natalie only stared at her. "I'm Mari, and will you look at that, I'm going to be late for my MRI, and you know they will give your spot away if you're late." Mari didn't even pretend to look at a clock. "Can you get away from your evil boss and walk me down?" she asked Davis, eyes twinkling.

"Go," Heather motioned, cleaning up the cards and getting out of the way.

"It was nice to meet you, Cason," Mari said as she walked backward on her crutches, making it look easy and almost choreographed. "I hope we can get everyone together before camp."

Cason just nodded in return. Because she could already see the ire building in Natalie Martin. It was the same look she wore if she thought Cason wasn't working hard enough.

"I know I've said I don't want you to be around that boy." Natalie's eyes drilled Cason. "And that *specialist*, she needs to stop pressuring us with this agenda."

"Agenda?"

"That ridiculous camp and group." Natalie refreshed her emails and opened a budget sheet. "And who was that girl?"

"Mari. She was nice." Cason didn't talk about how Mari was also terrifying. Okay, Mari herself wasn't terrifying, but her disability was Cason's worst nightmare.

"She's obviously an attention seeker."

"What?"

"Well, why else would she parade her disfigurement?"

"She's not disfigured." Cason's mouth dropped at the word. "She had cancer." But she didn't add *like me.* It sat on the tip of her tongue and in her throat, words that would be admittance confirmation of all the things she didn't want to admit. All that anxiety was starting to fill the empty crevices in her brain.

Natalie didn't say anything, but the words that Cason hadn't said reverberated between them, loudly echoing off the walls and slamming into each of them like a hurricane. Natalie's always-critical eyes tightened and told Cason exactly what her mother thought of everything. Cason was silent.

chapter seven

Davis wandered through the cafeteria on his way to the clinic. He knew that Cason was going to be there today, getting her second round of chemo. He also knew that this round would be a lot tougher on her than the other one. They had texted more and more over the past three weeks.

He washed toys, scraped Play-Doh off tables, bleached video game controllers, and restocked art supplies. He did exactly what he was supposed to do, but the entire time, he thought about Cason and what she might be doing.

Hopefully he'd killed enough time to not look too eager. He knocked on Cason's door, and Heather opened it slowly, letting him in. Cason was still sound asleep, her small body tucked into the brace. She looked sick. And not *I-have-a-cold* sick. He imagined that not even a person with the worst possible stomach virus could look as bad as Cason did right now.

"Vincristine is no joke, huh?" he said as Heather got Cason another wet washcloth. She let it rest around her neck, where it would hopefully help with the nausea.

"It's been rough," she agreed. "Natalie felt really bad about leaving, but Cason told her to go as she retched." Heather moved across the tiny room to Davis. "They've upped her usual anti-nausea as much as they can and finally gave her something that has a sedative too."

"She's green."

"Dr. Henderson said the same thing. I need to go eat, and I'm afraid if I do it here, it'll make her sick," Heather said.

"I can sit with her." Davis sat, scooting the chair closer toward her, resting a hand on hers.

Within five minutes, Cason stirred. He heard her moan, and he reached for the blue emesis bag, getting it to her just in time for her to start vomiting. She dry-heaved for a full minute before settling back in the bed.

"Sorry," she whispered hoarsely to him. Davis handed her the can of Sprite. It was what his mother had used when he was sick. "This is awful."

"Yep." He held the can for her as she finished. "It's okay. It happens to all of us."

"This is worse than the last time." Her words were so soft, he had to strain to hear her. "It's a good thing this is only a one-day treatment. There is no way I could do five."

"You could if you had to." He stroked a hand over her forehead. "Don't underestimate yourself."

"I'm sorry." She gagged over her words.

"You think I'm the first guy to hold a girl they like

while the girl pukes? Hell, I'd bet that half of prom court did the same thing this year."

She laughed then. It was small, but it was there. "I like you too, Davis."

She dozed more but Davis sat there, talking nonsense. He didn't think she was listening, but was sure that his talking somehow made her feel better. It gave him something else to think about other than the fact that:

A) She was currently puking whatever minuscule amount of stuff was left in her body

B) He'd told Cason that he liked her

C) And she'd said she liked him back.

~

Cason [6:01PM]: Yeah, I'm feeling better.

Davis [6:01PM]: Remember to take your meds on time and hopefully it'll help.

"Is this where the NA meeting is?" Alexis appeared on the steps just below Davis. He stumbled with surprise. "Hey."

"Hi." Davis could feel his heart pounding between his ears, surprise and fear filling his entire being. "Yeah, this is where the NA meeting is." He wanted to help Alexis make this change; after all, he'd been the one to help get her hooked in the first place.

"Am I supposed to be this scared?" She was shaking.

"The first step is the hardest." In every sense of the word, that had been true for Davis. Admitting he couldn't control anything in life, mostly his addiction, was something that he still struggled with even after months of sobriety. "But if I can do this, I know you can."

"Can you ever forgive me?" She twisted her fingers. They were cracked and the dried skin looked painful. "I've done so much to hurt you."

"Come on." He motioned for her to follow him in, but she just stood there, her curly locks twisting in the cool breeze of the late April evening.

"I'm so sorry, Davis." Then she bolted, turning on her heel and running down the stairs.

"Alexis!" he called after her, hoping he could get her to stop, to get her into the meeting. But she never stopped, never even looked at him.

Anxiety crawled up his spine, like tiny ant-like legs on his back. A premonition or a warning, or maybe just the incredibly deep and relentless need to get high. It ached within him, pulling at his gut and filling his lungs.

Before he could follow Alexis's lead and bolt, he trudged in through the old double doors of the church. The smell of decay and a building that needed repair took over the chemical smells in his brain.

The first steps were indeed the hardest.

The NA meeting seemed to drag on that night, or maybe Davis had more thoughts than usual running through his mind. The drugs had helped him forget, even for a brief time, that his real life had been a train wreck.

He hadn't been able to bear the strain of being a cancer survivor. Drugs had been an easy escape from that place.

"I would sit on the couch that my husband and I purchased together when we'd first gotten married and smoke pipe after pipe." Jacqueline No-Last-Name-Because-This-Was-Anonymous spoke. "This week, when my son threw a tantrum over a cheese stick, I could feel it again. I wanted to use.

"I didn't get high." Her smile was genuine. "Instead, I took Jonas out and we rode bikes."

"Thank you, Jacqueline." The meeting chairperson moved to the podium.

There was a mention of a new tea and a comment that the Daily Grind would supply the coffee for the next meeting. Then he led the group through the Serenity Prayer.

Davis closed his eyes and took a deep breath. In the beginning, he'd hated this part of the meetings. He felt like an impostor, pretending to be sober and functioning, when in reality, the only thing keeping him from getting high was the thought of jail time.

Now he was sober because he wanted to be. Now he wanted to stay that way.

He would reclaim himself. He would deal with life as it came at him.

~

Cason [7:24PM]: You're joking.
Davis [7:24PM]: No, for real. Dr. H is scared of needles.

Davis should not have been texting while he was leaving the meeting.

Davis [7:29PM]: Ask him what happened when he had to have his finger pricked.

"Channing."

Sometimes when your life is about to be irrevocably changed, your blood moves so slowly you can feel each slow, sluggish pump through your system.

The last time it had happened, he was arrested for possession of a controlled substance with intent to distribute.

This time, it was because the voice that had called his name had been the reason he'd had all those drugs on him to begin with.

"Ethan." Davis stopped, looking up from his phone. He measured how far it was to his car, but there was no way he could get to it. Not without having to go through Ethan first.

"I was hoping to run into you." Ethan stepped in. There were angry lines and a ruthless edge to him. Dark, greasy hair was plastered to his forehead and dark shadows filled in his eyes, making him even more terrifying. "I see you're still hanging around the NA scene. Some of my best clients are within those walls."

"You mean former clients." Panic made Davis stupid and a little too cocky.

"You're all still my clients, it's just a matter of time." Ethan stepped closer as Davis tried to get away. The acrid scent of him lingered, touching everything.

"I've got to be somewhere." Davis tried to move past. He just had to get past him, his car was right there. If he could just get around him.

Get away from Ethan.

Mixing together in his brain, he could feel panic and the pull of a high.

Instead of getting away, he could get high.

Yes ... The words whispered, filling his mouth, his brain, his nose. He didn't smell the dank alley or the restaurants nearby. He smelled chemicals, and could almost feel the relief of the high filling his senses.

A tight hand gripped his upper arm, holding him still. "Alexis says you're taking her debt." It brought him back to the very real present. Davis could still all but feel the glass pipe in his hand. Swallowing hard, he tried to clear the taste from his mouth.

"She's a dopehead. You can't believe anything she says." Davis spit on the ground, the taste lingering inside him. He tried to pull away again, but the hand tightened and four fingers were pushing into his muscle, bruising the skin.

"She says you work at the hospital. Maybe you can just get me some fentanyl. That would pay off her debt."

"You want me to get you fentanyl?" Davis laughed at the absurdity of this. "I don't even know where they keep that stuff."

"I can make it worth your time." Palmed in his hand was a small bag of pills.

The temptation of the high pulled at Davis's stomach in a visceral way.

YES! His heart rate picked up as he looked around, hoping that someone, anyone, was around to see him. Panic and anticipation pushed down his brain, down the back of his crushed throat, into his stomach, and coated it with heat and desire.

Just one time.

No one will know.

Just. One. More. Time.

There was the knife tucked inside the waist of Ethan's expensive jeans, side by side with the dope.

Both could kill him.

"I'm fine." Davis tried once again to get away, he had to get away. "I paid whatever debt I owed when I went to jail."

"You will always owe me." The grip on Davis's arm tightened. The knife that had been just a threat was now pressed just under his ribcage. There was a small trickle of blood, the heat of it slithered down over his stomach. "She owes me. You owe me." Davis barely registered the clanging in his brain as his skull cracked against the brick wall of the church. "I know your parents have money."

"Why are you all obsessed with my parents' money?" Talking was hard. "That doesn't mean I have any." The hand that wasn't pressing the knife to his skin was holding his throat nearly shut.

"You talk too much." New oxygen was in short supply. Ethan gripped his throat, pushing his windpipe back, making it impossible to talk or breathe. Davis could feel his legs moving, trying to strike purchase, his hands pulled on the ones around his neck, but the more he pulled, the harder it squeezed. Spots appeared in his vision and his breath was trapped into lungs.

Unable to escape.

Davis was unable to escape.

I should have gotten high.

Davis struggled, pushing, kicking, trying anything to get Ethan off him, but the ringing in his head was so loud, all he could think was *shut up!* If it would just shut up for a minute, he could get away. He felt a searing pain, more clanging in his skull, and then everything went blissfully dark.

chapter eight

Cason had finished her second round of chemo a little over a week ago. Now her blood counts were in the toilet. She could mostly tell because she felt like complete shit. Her energy was non-existent, and she was so pale that a vampire would be jealous.

Cason picked up her brush and began to rake it through her hair. She felt the tug and pull as her hair slid through the bristles . . . and out of her head.

There it was. There was the telltale sign that she was undergoing chemotherapy. She stared at the pink paddle brush and saw the strands of hair, her hair, hanging from the bristles. She touched it gingerly at first, then, pinching a few of the strands that were hanging from her head, she tugged.

It didn't hurt.

But there were those strands, perfectly long, like they had been cut, not pulled, from her.

It was just three long strands of blond hair.

But it felt like it was the last thing of her previous life that she'd had.

Her hair was just one more thing cancer was taking

from her. It wasn't enough that the cancer had taken her passion. It had to take this simple thing as well.

Cason debated if she should continue brushing it. She didn't even think of putting it up in a ponytail, afraid that it would all come out when she took it down. Instead, she crutched out of her bathroom. She carried her brush with her like a torch that proclaimed she was, in fact, going bald.

"Mom?"

Natalie sat at the breakfast bar, drinking her customary cup of black coffee, and looked up at her. It was plain to Cason that her mother had stopped sleeping. She was starting to look frayed. "Just a minute . . . This is Natalie." Her mom spoke into her phone. There was a pause, the air in the room changed. It thickened to the point that Cason couldn't breathe. It must be the hospital. She saw tears in her mom's eyes. She watched her move out of the room and farther away so that Cason couldn't hear her.

Cason was dying. She knew this because why else would her mom practically run to the other room? She had to be dying.

A few minutes later, Natalie reappeared, her eyes red from crying.

"What?" Cason could barely pull in a breath around the anxiety that lodged itself into her windpipe. "Was that the hospital?"

"No." Natalie pulled her into a hug. "It was New York."

"Oh." Cason didn't know how to process this

information. Her brain couldn't make the switch between the two worlds. New York meant dancing. And her brain couldn't go there.

"They were wondering how your injury was healing. I had to tell them you have a tumor."

"Oh." Her heart broke and dread trilled against her chest.

"And they let me know that they'd wanted you to join the Studio Company." Natalie sat next to her. She seemed to want to comfort Cason, but it was foreign to both of them now. "They were so impressed with you, with your talent."

Cason's breath stopped. She was in. The thing she had wanted most in her life. The dancing. The training in a city she loved. The prestige. All of it. It was hers.

But it wasn't.

None of it was hers and wouldn't be. She wouldn't step foot onto a stage or in a dance studio this summer. She would spend it at a hospital. She wouldn't even get to tie on her pointe shoes.

"But I have cancer." She looked up at her mother, trying to make sense of all of this. "I'm not going to dance anywhere."

"I'm so sorry, Cason." And then her mom, the unbreakable Natalie Martin, was crying. Not gut-wrenching sobs or anything like that, but sad tears streamed down her elegant face. Cason couldn't think of a time when she'd seen her mother cry in her entire life.

"I have cancer." Tears streamed. Panic was rising in the back of her throat like an uncoiling snake, slowly filling her airway. "I have cancer. And how can I dance when I have cancer and my leg is in a brace because my bone is mush?" She gulped air, but nothing controlled the sobs. "This is not supposed to be my life."

~

Later that morning, Cason waited in the exam room, grateful for a door that closed. She didn't want to deal with people. She wanted to sit in her little cubicle and sulk. Tears of self-pity trailed down her cheeks. The tears stung; she hated feeling so sorry for herself. But it didn't make the feelings any easier.

"Tough morning, Cason?" Heather walked in, arms loaded with magazines. "I saw your mom leave, so I figured some company might be needed."

"My hair is falling out." She had been swallowing down the hard lump, turning her voice to gravel. She couldn't talk about the offer from ABT yet, the way that her world had almost been perfect. "I know it's stupid, but—"

"It's not stupid." Heather sat next to her, handing her a magazine and pair of safety scissors. "Cut out nature pictures. I'd normally make Davis do this, but he's got school or something."

"Okay." Cason flipped through the magazine and saw pictures of waterfalls and butterflies.

"How are you feeling?" Heather pulled a page from her own magazine, but it only had a really fantastic coat on it. "What? I need a new coat."

"It's just hair. It'll grow back." Cason tried to find some conviction in her words.

"Cason, in the past two months, you've had to undergo more change and pain than you ever have in your entire life." Heather offered her some understanding. "You get to be upset about this. You get to feel mad because your hair is falling out. Who cares if it's just hair? It's your hair and you can be sad about it."

"It does get easier, right?" she sniffed.

"You bet," Heather said. "You know that cliché saying about life being a marathon, not a sprint?"

"Yes. I always thought it was annoying."

"Just go with the analogy for me. This is like, mile fourteen. You're past the halfway mark where until now it's been mostly easy and flat. Now you're running straight up a mountain and it's going to be this way until mile twenty."

"So, I only have to run six miles uphill."

"That's right. But, don't think a sweet, flat-ish mountain. Think something in the Rockies, or better yet the Himalayas."

"Awesome." Cason dried her cheeks.

"And it might not feel like it, but you do have some control here." Heather cut out a lizard and stuffed it into the folder she brought. It was brimming with pictures, leading Cason to think this was really a way of distracting her. "I just want you to think about this. No need to make a decision right now, but you could shave your head."

"What?" Cason was now very sure that Heather was terrible at her job. "Why would I want to do that?"

"Listen, it's going to fall out anyway. This way, you get to say when." Heather hopped off the exam table, taking her magazines and folder with her. "Just think about it."

~

"How are you feeling, Cason?" Dr. Henderson stood close to the exam table, but didn't pick up any instruments yet. He folded his hands in front of him like they were having a friendly conversation.

"Fine." She shrugged. "Tired, I guess."

"Your blood counts have taken a hit, which is exactly what should happen at this point after chemo." He picked up the otoscope, placing the protective cap on it, and began the exam. "Given your numbers, I'd like you to come in tomorrow for a blood transfusion. That'll help with your energy as well."

"Her hair has started falling out." Natalie was sitting on the edge of her seat, her left foot vibrating with nerves. "Is that normal? I thought it wouldn't happen until after another round of chemotherapy."

"Her counts are very low. It's to be expected." Dr. Henderson smiled and attempted to warm up the stethoscope by rubbing it on the outside of his white coat, before placing it on Cason's back. "Deep breath. Has Heather talked to you about shaving your head?"

"What?" Natalie's mouth fell open, like a fish, and Cason had the strangest urge to laugh. "Why would she ever do that?"

"It's just something she sometimes offers to patients." Dr. Henderson smiled before facing Cason again to continue the conversation. "It's up to you, of course."

"Yeah, she mentioned it." Cason pulled at little pieces of the paper covering the exam table, tearing it into tiny bits of confetti.

"That's completely ridiculous." Natalie was almost on her feet. Cason could practically feel her need to pace the room. "Why would Cason want to look like she has . . . is sick?" She quickly corrected the words.

Dr. Henderson smiled at Cason, his brows furrowed a little as he tapped on the bones of her sinuses. "How's that? Sore?"

"No," Cason said. "Should it be?" She immediately began to panic just a little.

"Not unless you're sick." He smiled. "I'll want you to come back in tomorrow." He pulled out his tablet and made some notations.

"Because I need a transfusion." The words were sticky in her throat, but she didn't want to let her doctor know that the idea of the transfusion made her incredibly nervous.

"Yes." He smiled. "You're catching on. I saw you met Mari."

"She was . . . impressive." Cason wasn't sure whether that was the right word. "She walks really smoothly."

"She's been on crutches a lot longer than you have." Dr. Henderson moved toward the door, preparing to leave. "But she'd be someone good for you to talk to."

"Right." Natalie huffed the word. "Thank you, Doctor."

"Natalie, you can speak with the schedulers about what time to bring Cason in for her transfusion."

"He was full of unhelpful advice today," Natalie said once he was out of earshot. She scooped up their belongings and shoved everything into the oversized Kate Spade bag they now lived out of. "That girl has nothing in common with you."

"Except we both have cancer."

"Hers was obviously much worse." The unsaid *she's missing a leg!* was implied. "And why would you ever shave your head?"

This wasn't a conversation. It was a monologue so Natalie could repeat her opinions out loud and Cason could nod in agreement.

"Can I borrow Cason for a moment?" Heather slid up to them a moment later as Natalie waited to schedule her appointment for the next day. "There's a celebrity over in the main lobby of the hospital." She smiled beguilingly at Natalie.

"I'll meet you there if I ever get this done." Natalie scrolled through her email, irritation and impatience all over her face.

Heather didn't wait for Natalie, just stuffed Cason into a wheelchair and cackled like she'd just done the best thing ever.

"Where are we going in such a hurry?" Cason almost felt like laughing again.

"Shh." Heather tucked the crutches beside Cason in the wheelchair.

"Heather . . ." Cason drawled out her name.

"So, we're a children's hospital, right?" Heather continued to look around, her excitement obvious.

"I have yet to see an adult in one of the embarrassing hospital gowns."

"Well, sometimes celebrities come and visit. And it appears that the pitcher from the Braves, you know the cute one? Not the one with the awful ERA, the one who just came up from AAA last year, yeah, he's here."

"And you need me why?"

"The hospital frowns on staff hogging celebrities' time when they are technically visiting patients and stuff."

"You're using me for my cancer status."

"If you got it, flaunt it."

A loud, honest laugh erupted from Cason. It felt as good as the tears from earlier. Heather was off, gathering more kids to meet the baseball player, and Cason was sitting off to the side, observing. She didn't have a real desire to meet this guy, but would for Heather's sake.

She watched people, young girls and boys with their caps in hand, nurses trying to appear to be helpful, but really doing the same thing Heather was. But instead of sneaking in an autograph, Heather had disappeared. When she finally returned, she was no longer excited about a baseball player. Her face was drawn with seriousness, her expressive eyes subdued.

"Come with me." Heather helped her stand. "Can you walk?"

"Sure." Cason didn't argue, just went with her. They headed down a few hallways and into the elevator to the first floor. "Why are we here?" They walked down the inpatient unit that was for observation, usually for kids who had been transferred from the emergency department.

"Davis was admitted."

chapter nine

Davis didn't know how he got to the hospital, just that he was waking up to that familiar sterile smell and pure oxygen. Through the cracks of the curtain partitioning off his room, he saw his parents talking to a police officer. His mother's arms were wrapped around herself, while his father's hands were braced behind his head and his cheeks were puffed out. The worry line he'd given his mother during his diagnosis, the one that had only become more prominent when she'd checked him into rehab, was back.

An IV pulled at his hand, a nasal cannula burned his nose, and he had a pounding headache. He remembered exactly what happened before he woke up in the hospital. He thought about sitting up, but the stinging coming from his ribs told him that it was not a good idea. Instead, he laid there and thought about what he would tell the police. He was sure they had already run a drug test. It would show he was sober. He knew he had some sort of pain medication circulating through him. His head felt funny, or maybe that was the concussion.

"Davis?" His mom ran a comforting hand over his head, soothing him.

"I'm here. Sort of."

"You're going to be fine. A concussion, bruised ribs, stitches." She swept his hair off his forehead, her fingers cool on his skin. "They didn't hit anything too important."

"That explains the pain in my chest," His words were slow, "and the numbness in my stomach."

"Were you mugged?"

"Something like that."

"Let him sleep." It was his dad, sounding stern and harsh, but the fact that his hand gripped Davis's told him it wasn't directed at him, only the situation. "We'll have time to talk about it later."

When he woke up again, he wasn't sure how much later it was. It could have been ten minutes or ten hours. Heather guided his parents away, and Cason was left standing there. She was next to his bed, holding the hand that didn't have an IV in it. She looked over her shoulder, then back to him, and flashed a wobbly smile. The feeling of her hand was so real, but he couldn't be sure this wasn't a drug-induced dream.

"Want me to go get the nurse?" Her words were rushed, worried.

"No." He swallowed painfully, feeling as if he had been sleeping with his mouth wide open. "Do I look as bad as I feel?"

Her shoulders relaxed and she squeezed his hand softly. "You do look pretty bad. You probably look worse than me and I'm the one who has cancer. And my hair has started falling out."

"You look better than you did when I saw you last week." He looked at her. Her hair was down but didn't appear to be any different than any other time he'd seen it. "And you can't tell about your hair."

"Yet." She drew the word out, getting a laugh from him.

He wanted to tell her that bald was beautiful, he wanted to tell her that it wouldn't matter because she would still have those killer eyes, but then he realized that he had massive amounts of pain medication coursing through his body, which might mean he had already said these things. The smile that spread across her face was sweet and a little embarrassed. "I guess I said all of that out loud."

"What happened?" Her words were quiet, as she changed the subject. "If you want to tell me."

"You know how we were taught to stand up to bullies in elementary school?" he asked.

She nodded.

"Sometimes when you stand up to those bullies, they have friends who will beat you up."

"Someone you know did this to you?"

"I'm clean." He sounded more drugged out now than he had when he was using. "Well, minus the painkillers I was given." He winced then and touched his ribs. "I have been clean and sober for eight months. Being an addict is hard and something I have to fight against every single day." He swallowed, letting the pain ease. "Some people think I owe them."

"People you know did this to you?" She repeated the question, with wide eyes and slightly parted lips, filling the room with her disbelief.

He cringed as he spoke. "I was grabbed after my NA meeting"

"Why?"

"Money." He sighed.

"Davis, you have to tell the police."

"I haven't decided what to do yet." A burn gnarled around in his stomach. Whatever local anesthetic that had been used to stitch him up was wearing off. He'd been stabbed. He let that thought sit in his damaged brain. He'd been stabbed and beaten by someone who had once sold him drugs.

His ribs ached and his brain thrummed with a ticking pain. He tried to breathe through the pain, but that just made it worse. A sharp jolt rang through the bones of his ribs with each cleansing breath he attempted to take.

"Davis." It was a plea. "They really hurt you." Her voice was heavy with concern.

"I know." The current thunder rolling through his brain and skull reminded him.

Cason was getting ready to say more, he could see the words forming on her lips, but she was cut off as Heather came back in the room.

"We'll talk later, Davis," Heather smiled. "About a lot of things." She raised an eyebrow, and Cason blushed deeply.

"I'm sure you have a lot to tell me." He hadn't sounded this bad even when he had been on chemo.

"I've got to get Cason back before her mom sends the guards." Heather pulled the wheelchair in.

"Think about it, Davis." Cason squeezed his hand once more. It took a bit for Cason to get situated in the chair with her crutches and monstrous brace. "We'll talk more later too."

"Don't be nice to him, Cason." Heather tried to sound stern, but the kindness in her eyes completely nullified her words.

"Don't tell Dr. H," Davis sat up as much as his body would let him. "I can't handle a visit from him too."

"That man knows all." Heather said, backing out of the room with Cason. "I'm sure he's already talked to the ER docs and the neurologist."

"Well, tell him I'm okay."

"I will if I run into him," Cason said.

"Back to the clinic," Heather jumped in before things could get any more intense.

The police came in next. They wanted to talk. Davis didn't know if he was up to talking then, or if he ever would be. He was still on probation, he could still go to jail if he slipped up and broke any part of that probation. In his past experiences, the cops were rarely on his side of things. And he didn't know whether they would be now.

chapter Ten

Cason shuddered, watching someone else's blood drip into her. She tried to get lost in the movie playing on her TV. She was out in the fishbowl surrounded by others also getting an infusion. Their presence was all that kept her from freaking out.

Davis [11:45AM]: At the clinic?

Cason thanked God for his timing. Davis's text could hopefully keep her from having the panic attack she could feel coming on. Happy nerves filled her stomach. They hadn't discussed what he'd said the other day. His admission to the hospital had stalled any flirting that might have been happening. Cason had little experience to draw on, so she thought he was flirting. Or maybe he was just being nice.

Cason [11:45AM]: Yeah, my counts are in the toilet. I'm getting a transfusion.
Davis [11:46AM]: I'm being discharged. I'll be by after lunch.
Cason [11:46AM]: I don't think I'm going anywhere. Thnx.
Davis [11:47AM]: We'll talk.
Cason [11:47AM]: Good. I'll start brainstorming topics so I don't freak out about the blood.

Davis [11:47AM]: Get Heather to cover it. Then you can't see it.
Cason [11:48AM]: I'm not 4, that won't help.
Davis [11:48AM]: Trust me. I'll see you in a few.

All she wanted was for someone to distract her from the blood. She tried to focus on Davis. How he'd looked yesterday. How he'd told her about what happened. Cason's thoughts meandered, moving from one point to another, but the one thing she focused on was that she didn't feel nervous around Davis like she did the other guys at school. He always seemed to want to make her happy. Or maybe that was her long-dormant hormones making her think that.

Drip. Drip. Drip.

She had to stay hooked up to the blood pressure cuff to make sure that she wasn't having an adverse reaction to the transfusion, which did nothing for her anxiety levels. Heather came walking in with a deck of Uno cards and a pillowcase that was decorated with some sorority letters. "I have cards and a blood bag cover."

"How did you know?" She breathed in and out, counting the exhale. "I don't think it'll help."

"I know all. I also know you've been texting with Davis this morning. Your champion told me you might need a little something." One brow raised and her words teased.

"Are you trying to distract me?"

"Is it working?" Heather was sliding the pillowcase over the blood and sat down to deal out the cards. "Plus, I like to think I had a little to do with this new couple."

"New couple?" Cason almost gagged, but she was sure that was because of the blood.

"Sure." Heather wiggled her eyebrows.

"Whatever." She huffed. "He was letting me know that he would drop by after he was discharged." Cason scanned her cards, looking for one that would shut Heather up. "He's being nice."

"Oh, is that what it's called these days when a guy makes sure to come by the hospital he's being checked out of after he's been beaten up to the point of an admission?" Heather played her cards. "My husband is never that nice to me."

"Aren't you supposed to be helping me? Did you forget your job?"

"You know, if you go to camp this year, you could spend a whole week with him. Only the eyes of us counselors watching."

"Heather, I'm too old to go." Even the idea of spending the week away from her mom could not entice her to spend it instead at a camp full of kids with cancer. "Maybe when I'm older, I can be a counselor or something."

"You can do both, experience camp as a camper and then as a counselor."

"We'll see." It was as close to a commitment she was going to get. She had no desire to spend a week talking about cancer. On top of that, she was sick. She had blood dripping into her right now. She would have more chemo and probably surgery before this camp.

"Did Davis tell you what happened?"

"What?" Cason had been so lost in her own thoughts that she had almost forgotten Heather was even there.

"Did he tell you what happened the other day?"

"He got beat up." She played a red six on a green six and watched as Heather drew several cards before being able to play.

"He did tell you."

"Yes, he told me." Cason played a draw four and changed the color to yellow. "I'm hoping he's told his parents."

"He didn't tell them first?"

"He hadn't told anyone." Cason shuffled, reorganizing the cards as she planned her move. "He doesn't know me all that well. I don't know why he'd tell me."

"Maybe it's because he *doesn't* know you." Heather easily had fifteen cards in her hand right now. Cason assumed she could play at least one yellow card.

"All I really know about him was that he'd dated Alexis Foster. Heather, I didn't even go to our school for full days because of dance, half my day was at the studio."

"And now?"

"My life now consists of chemotherapy, blood trans-fusions, and the very real possibility that I will never dance again." Her throat closed over the words. She still couldn't think about her ABT invitation. Especially when it was now going to someone else. "I can stand to make a couple friends." Her voice lost all volume, becoming a whisper.

Heather stopped then, looking up at Cason from her cards. She reached out and took Cason's hand in hers, looking as though she wanted to make sure that what she was about to say was really heard, not just glossed over.

"Cason, you might not dance the way you did, but you can always dance again. Two legs, one leg, no legs. Dance is a part of who you are and you will find it again."

Cason didn't answer. Her heart was held together by tiny threads. Even thoughts about not ever doing a *grand jeté* or a *tendu* could sever them. In her dreams at night, she could leap and *bourrée* across the floor with one leg. It was as if her other leg no longer existed at all. She always woke up a little more broken, with a little more of her previous life gone.

"I have a proposition for you." Heather broke their respective silence.

"I'm not being your ticket to meet another athlete. You realize I only know the vague difference between football and baseball, right?"

"I know that I'm going to have to spend some time brainwashing you about sports stars, but that's not what this is about."

Cason's stomach turned a little bit, hoping the proposition wouldn't have something to do with Davis or camp. She didn't want to break Davis's confidence, but she didn't know how to skate around these questions much longer. "Okay, what is it?"

"I have an electric razor here."

"Okay." That had nothing to do with Davis.

"So, if you want to shave your head, you can."

"Oh, you weren't kidding about that."

"Take some control." Heather put down her cards and reclined back as if she was going to nap, not discuss Cason's hair.

Thoughts were dancing through her head so fast she couldn't grasp any. Mostly her mind repeated *Bald* ad nauseam. "Some control would be nice." The slow words contrasted with her heart rate.

"This is one way to get some." There was a pause and Heather's brow arched slowly, this time with a mischievous grin. "Seriously, you can control this." Cason looked at her doubtfully. "You can't control the fact that your hair is going to fall out. Nothing is going to stop it now, but you can control how and when it happens. You can let it happen slowly and then be left with a few strange stragglers that I've seen little girls insist on putting into ponytails. Or you can make it a clean break. Like ripping off a Band-Aid."

Cason could take this one matter of her cancer into her own hands and literally *do* something about it.

"I'll bet you a game of Uno." Davis materialized out of nowhere. One second, it was just her and Heather, and now, suddenly, he was there, challenging her to a game of Uno. "If I win, you shave your head."

"And if I win?"

"You don't have to shave your head." He sent her a crooked grin, one that had been popping up in her mind more often lately. It was only slightly marred by the disgusting bruise that covered his eye and ran up into his hair. The purple and red streaks were partially covered by a bandage just below his hairline. He didn't move fast, that was for sure, but sat down slowly, holding his side as he did.

"Where did you come from?" Heather seemed just as mystified as Cason.

"First floor. They finally released me."

"And you're still choosing to stay at the hospital." Heather shook her head in pretend confusion. "Davis, I doubt I'll ever understand you."

"Most don't, so I'm not too concerned." He leaned forward, his eyes still swollen, the impishness barely visible. "You up for it? Or are you chicken?"

"I'll play."

"You have to go through with it if I win. No backing down."

"I never back down." Cason felt her eyes narrow as Heather cackled with excitement. She dealt the cards to ensure no cheating happened, even though Cason argued she was on Davis's side. But everyone playing the game knew that Cason was going to end this day bald.

The game was heated. It was full of reverses, draw two, draw fours, and plenty of extra pick-ups. Cason actually almost won on more than one occasion, but she kept forgetting to call Uno when she had one card left. Davis would get her every time, making her draw four more. In the end, they each had two cards left. Cason could go out if the color stayed yellow. She desperately needed the color to stay yellow. She held her breath as Davis laid down his card. It was yellow. Her breath had almost escaped until she saw that it was a skip a turn. And since it was only the two of them, he skipped her and then went right out on a yellow four.

Davis helped her stand, handing her crutches. "Let's do this."

"Now?" Cason asked incredulously.

Heather pushed Cason's IV pole over toward her office. "We'll do it in here. I'll put down some paper."

"I still have blood dripping into me!"

"We'll take everything with us." Heather started pushing the IV pump.

"I'll tell your nurse," Davis commented. "You'll need a mirror. You go set up your office while I find one."

Cason watched as they moved around for her. Davis was still moving pretty slowly and holding onto his ribs, but he didn't seem nearly as out of it as he had yesterday. She wanted to talk to him more about what happened. But first, she had to shave her head.

Her mother would be pissed. And that was the right incentive, it seemed.

"You ready?" Heather propped a mirror on her desk and spread a sheet over the floor to catch her hair. "Do you want to keep your hair or toss it?"

"Toss it." Cason said without thinking. "I won't need it anymore."

The buzz of the razor was one of the most frightening sounds Cason had heard in recent memory. She held it in her hands and could feel the vibrations shake nearly her entire arm. She wasn't sure she could do this.

The room was silent except for the buzz of the razor and the breaths of the three people in the office. She looked in the mirror. She was Cason Martin. She could do anything, shaving her own head included. As if her hand was moving through water, she lifted up the razor. Slowly, she moved it over her head, surprised by the friction she met at the side of her head, where her hair got tangled. But it didn't stop her. She shook off the hair and continued to work, shaving off patches at a time. Lightness began to fill her lungs as each lock hit the floor. She couldn't stop this. Her hair was falling out, and this way, she owned some of it.

"Cason!" It was her mother's voice, strained and shaking.

"Hi, Mom!" She looked over, hair falling everywhere, a giggle turning into a full out laugh. "What do you think of my new haircut?"

chapter Eleven

The sheer joy currently covering Cason's face was so beautiful. He always wanted her to look this happy. But the frustration, or maybe even fear, that filled her mother's eyes was just as appealing. Cason deserved a little rebellion, and this was a perfect place to start.

"What are you doing?" Mrs. Martin seethed out the words through her perfectly straight, ultra-white teeth. They were probably veneers.

"I'm taking control." Cason was gleeful as the razor ran over another patch of scalp, leaving her with wisps of hair and strands hanging from every direction. This was not some clean, movie-perfect shave. Hair was everywhere, and she was constantly having to stop to clean out the blades. No sad or overly heroic music played as she cut her hair either, just the buzz of the clippers, and the cackle of her slightly off-kilter laugh.

"You missed a spot." He pointed to right behind her left ear. "If you leave it, you could be a trendsetter."

"Was it really falling out that bad?" Natalie looked at Heather, refusing to look at him.

"It's just hair." Cason smiled.

"It helps them take control of what is going on in their

lives," Heather explained patiently. Davis suspected that some of this was true, maybe a lot of it, but it also made things easier. Davis had gotten a buzz cut, something his mother had never allowed before, and he'd loved those first few weeks without hair. He wondered how Cason would feel.

"Cason, you didn't have to do this." Natalie was desperate.

"Yes, yes, I did."

"You lost a bet," Davis reminded her.

"A bet? You made a bet?" Natalie's voice inched up by decibels with each word.

"The cancer can't take this from me. I get to be the one in charge of how and when and where my hair falls out." Cason breathed then and looked over at Davis, who was doing his best to be there and not in the way. "Will you get the back for me?"

"Absolutely." Mischief and laughter filled her as he took the razor.

"I'm going to find Dr. Henderson." Natalie's voice shook. "You'll be lucky if either of you have a job after this." The only sound after that was the clacking of Natalie's heels and the buzz of the razor.

Davis picked up locks of the blond hair off the floor. "Are you sure you don't want to keep any of it? Posterity and whatnot?"

Cason seemed to think about it, touching the top of her head and around her ears, which seemed more prominent to him now. Then she met his gaze through the mirror. Without her hair, her eyes were striking. "Nope. I'm not keeping it." She kicked it with the toe of her one foot and then smiled at him. "Did you see the look on my mom's face?"

Heather laughed, helping clean some of the hair off Cason and supporting her on her crutches. "I'm hoping that Davis and I still have jobs tomorrow."

"She can't really get you fired, can she?" Cason looked stricken.

"No," Heather assured. "You're not the first person to shave their head in my office. Second, your mom has earned quite the reputation."

"She can be . . . demanding," Cason apologized.

Davis snorted. "That's being kind."

"She wants the best for you." Heather cut in. The trio made their way back toward the treatment area. It was big and open, with clusters of recliners sectioned off by curtains and a perimeter of private rooms on the outside usually reserved for kids getting chemo. There were several big, round tables around the room where patients and siblings could play games or make crafts during the long visits. Davis wasn't entirely convinced that Natalie Martin wanted the best for anyone other than Natalie Martin. He wondered what it would take for Cason to become the center of her life.

"Davis." He turned to see Dr. Henderson standing there, his gray hair shaggy and nearly hanging in his glasses. "Let's go to exam room four. I want to look at those ribs and stitches myself."

"I'll meet you." He walked over to Cason. He noticed that Heather had magically disappeared into the staff break room, claiming she needed a soda. Davis would have to get her something for her convenient disappearing act. "The new haircut works." His fingertips brushed the now-bald skin above her ear. He took a step closer, able to feel her quick breaths.

The blush that filled her cheeks was instantaneous and rare. He'd never seen her blush before. "Thanks for beating me at Uno."

"Don't let your mom get you down, okay?" He held her gaze for a beat. "She doesn't get it. Cason. She's fighting what's happening."

"This was good for me." She chewed her lip, and rogue tears filled her eyes. "I found out yesterday that I was invited to join the Studio Company at the American Ballet Theatre. They invited me knowing that I'd had an injury." He didn't care how much it hurt his ribs. He moved into her, wrapping his arms around her in a hug, careful to keep them both balanced. "I was auditioning when my leg gave out. It's the one thing I've wanted my entire life."

"Cason." The soft down of what was left of her hair just touched his cheek. "That is just..." He paused. "I don't really have the right vocabulary for how lousy that is."

"Right?" She sniffed hard, but he could feel the tears

on his shirt. "The timing and everything." She pulled back from him, just enough that he could see her face. "But, I can deal with my mom, Davis." Her mouth turned up a little more, a small laugh. "Can you deal with Dr. Henderson or should I fake an emergency?"

"You fake something and it'll land you in the hospital." He shook his head. He reminded himself that her counts were low, too low for him to be this close, and that he should back away. That he should stop all thoughts of wanting to kiss her right now.

"Dr. H is going to send out the nurses." Cason's voice was soft, a little rough, and did nothing to stop all the thoughts in his concussed brain.

"Right." Slowly, he let her go.

Davis went to exam room four where Dr. Henderson was already waiting. "Doc."

"Davis. On the table." Davis slowly pulled himself up. The stitches pulled, and his bruised ribs shouted in pain with each movement. "I've seen your CT scan and your x-rays. You're lucky, kid."

"I take a lickin' and keep on tickin'."

"You're too young to have ever seen that commercial." Dr. Henderson's eyes laughed, even if he didn't.

"It's from a commercial?"

Dr. H insisted on poking him in the ribs, which caused him to suck in air. "Hurt?"

"Yep."

"They sutured you up nicely. This could have been

much worse." He probed gently around the knife wound. "You have some pretty nasty bruises, son."

"It feels that way."

"Any chance you want to tell me how you acquired these?"

Davis knew the request wasn't optional. He studied his hands for a minute, the only bruise there one from the IV he'd had the night before. Cason was still the only one who knew the whole truth, and he was beginning to feel guilty about that. So, with a deep breath, he started from the top of the story.

"This guy, Ethan. I used to score from him." He breathed out again, thankful that the doctor had stopped his exam. "I was set up by my ex. She told him that I could repay her debt to him. They both seem to think I owe them something."

Dr. Henderson believed Davis, which wasn't something Davis deserved after the crap he had pulled a year ago. "What are your plans, Davis?"

"I don't know. My parents only know bits and pieces of the story because I didn't want them to worry." Davis sat up slowly and let his legs hang off the paper-covered table. The bright primary colors of the clinic did nothing for his head.

"Need I remind you how hard I worked to keep you alive when you had cancer? I don't want to have to worry about you now that you're healthy."

"I know." Davis groaned.

"And you are doing great, Davis." Dr. Henderson never failed to mention how far he'd come. "So, what happens if you tell the police exactly what happened?"

"I'm guessing they'd have to find some evidence or something? I'm not sure exactly. I haven't talked to the cops."

"Why?"

"Who would they believe? I have a record."

"You also have people who would vouch for you. What's the worst that will happen?"

Davis thought about that. He'd have to deal with more questions. "I don't want to go through with all of it if I won't be believed."

"You were obviously assaulted, Davis. They have to listen to you when you say this is who did it." Dr. Henderson looked up then from Davis's chart, and there was truth in his eyes. "I'll want to see you when they take the stitches out, but right now, you're okay." Dr. H smiled gently at him. "Go, I've got actual sick kids to see."

"Thanks." Davis slid off the exam table slowly and left the room.

He knew Dr. H was right. But it didn't change the turning in his stomach when he thought of going to the police. Davis didn't want to go find his mom just yet, so he walked down the hall back toward the fishbowl. And if Cason just happened to be there, bonus.

"What did Dr. Henderson say?" Cason demanded the second he appeared.

"He checked over my ribs and stomach, which hurt." He tried to get some sympathy, but it didn't deter her interrogation.

"What did you tell him about the attack?"

"You can't keep secrets from Dr. H. I've tried. So, I told him the truth." He chewed on the cuticle of his nail, the dull ache in his skull beginning to steal his thoughts. "But, honestly, I just want to pretend none of it happened."

"But you were assaulted." Worry coated her words.

He liked the fact that Cason didn't really remember him when he was doped up, that she had known vaguely who he was, but only had true memories where he was sober. This whole thing just reminded him that he could never escape his past. "If I forget, then I can keep pretending that I'm not an addict." He paused. Davis looked at her, at those lovely blue eyes, brilliant against her white skin. "But I am."

"You're Davis." Cason said. "Let's make a deal." She was smiling, and it didn't exactly comfort him. "If I win this round of Uno, you go to the police and tell them everything. If you win, you can continue to wrestle with it until you find a way to get out of it."

"A game of Uno?"

"It did help with my new hairdo." She ran a hand over her mostly bald scalp. "Not having to make the decision was sort of nice. Let me see if I can repay the favor."

"Fine. If you win, I go to the police and tell them what

happened. If I win, I'll still think about doing that, but you can't pester me anymore."

"Fair." It wasn't as intense as the hair-loss game. If he lost, then the decision was made for him and he didn't have to think about it anymore.

"Want to tell me what Dr. Henderson said about all of this?" she asked.

"The same thing you did." Davis played a two, happy to get rid of a card.

"And what are you thinking?"

"That I wouldn't necessarily mind losing." He looked up at her. The electricity in the air was palpable. And it had nothing to do with the bet or the game, and everything to do with whatever chemistry was coming off each of them.

He only had two cards left. He could probably win the game with this move, but did he want to? He looked at Cason, looked at his cards, and decided that he didn't want to win. He needed to talk to the police for himself too. He needed this last bit of closure about that time in his life.

"Thanks for being my friend."

The word friend was good, but it didn't seem quite adequate to him. Or maybe he just thought there was more. "Of course. I know what it's like. I know how your world starts orbiting on a different axis than everyone else's, so I wanted to, I don't know . . . be nice." He played a card on hers. "That, and I really like watching your

102

mom get annoyed. She turns purple." He didn't mention that Cason was gorgeous and that he had been plotting reasons to hang out with her.

"Wonder what she'll do when she finds out we're . . ." She searched for a word. "Friends?" Cason played her last card. Davis took her outstretched hand, stroking his thumb over the sensitive skin on the inside of her wrist.

"Maybe we're more than friends." Davis winced, feeling awkward about everything, but he really couldn't help but smile.

"Maybe." Cason's smile said yes.

"I'll call you after I talk to my parents." He held her gaze for another moment before letting go.

"I don't have much on my social calendar these days. I think I can work you in."

"I hate to break up the lovefest, but Cason, your mom is heading this way and I'm not sure she wants to see much of Davis right now," Heather said, walking past them and heading to another patient with a stack of coloring books and markers.

"She's right. She's probably already tried to get me fired from my volunteer job," Davis said.

"Probably." Cason smiled.

"Thanks, Cason." He stood, needing to step away before he kissed her, low counts be damned.

"I'm glad I could help. Now get out of here. We've made my mom angry enough for one day."

He turned back once, out of range where Mrs. Martin

could see him, but where he could still see Cason. She was pale, she was bald, and she looked sick, but at that moment, she was the most beautiful person in the world.

chapter Twelve

There was no conversation on the car ride home, only deep huffs, and a simmering anger that radiated off her mom. Cason tried not to relish in it too much, but her entire life, she had been the perfect daughter, and for the first time ever, she'd done something that she had wanted to do without her mother's strict approval.

"Mom, it's just hair."

Still silence. It was heavy and intensified in the pressure cooker the car had become.

"Seriously, it was going to fall out anyway. I did something about it on my own."

After a prolonged stretch of tense silence, Natalie tersely began to speak. "I thought we agreed this was not going to interfere with your life."

"Wait, what?" Cason wanted to twist to see her mom better in her seat, but the brace kept her from moving too much. "Not interfere with my life?"

"Yes. This is just a stupid inconvenience and will be done in less than a year." Natalie's knuckles turned white around the steering wheel.

"And then what?" Cason wanted to laugh. "I just start dancing again? Pick up at ABC like I'd never left?"

"Exactly."

"Mom. I. Have. CANCER." She said each word as if it was its own sentence. "You have to understand what that means." Was this some weird alternate universe where Natalie Martin wasn't a competent woman who managed one of the most prestigious ballet conservatories in the United States?

"I am aware of your diagnosis, Cason."

"Really? Because you haven't ever said the word." Cason's voice was quiet, almost silent.

"What do you mean?" Natalie never looked at Cason, just focused on the road ahead. "What word?"

"Cancer."

The word hung in the air between them, hovering around like a putrid smoke cloud. The silence stretched, uncomfortable and unavoidable.

"I've said it."

"No, you haven't." They parked in their spacious, two-car garage. Cason's used Civic sat in its spot. She could remember exactly the last time she drove it. "With you, it's a 'tumor' or 'disease.' Never cancer. Never the 'C' word." She made no move to get out of the car.

"You're being dramatic." Natalie flung the door open and escaped the car like it was sinking into the ocean.

But Natalie still had to come around and help Cason out. Getting in and out of the car was one of the many things that she could no longer do on her own. Cason slowly walked into the kitchen, wishing she had the grace of Mari and the words that Davis seemed to always have.

"I have said it, numerous times now." They stood in the kitchen, almost at an impasse. "Cason, I know you think I'm hard on you because I'm your mom."

"Actually, I've always assumed you were hard on me because you were my artistic director." The nastiness that leaked out of her voice was so heavy that it coated the floor.

"I deserve that." Natalie poured a glass of wine, an irregular occurrence: too many empty calories. "I pushed you harder than the rest of the dancers because I always expected you to be the best."

"It didn't matter what I wanted."

"No, it didn't." Natalie didn't try to argue. "I always knew you would be a principal with the American Ballet Theatre."

"I wanted that too."

"Still want it," Natalie demanded. "You are still going to be a dancer, Cason."

She stopped her mother with a look. "I'm not thinking past my next chemo treatment."

"I do not want you associating with Davis Channing or his friends. This camp he attends is morbid." Natalie changed the subject, clearly unable to argue with Cason about the other subject.

Cason was quiet as she processed her mother's words.

"Mom, Davis and his friends, they are the only people in this world who completely understand what this is like."

"I'm here!" she yelled, losing her composure. "I understand."

"No, no you don't." Tears of anger flooded Cason's eyes, and she wiped at them furiously. "You can't accept any of this. I have cancer, Mom. I have a gross, disgusting form of cancer, and the only way to treat it is to give me poison. Poison that takes my strength, my hair." She stopped, tears of hurt and pain choking her. "And dance," she finally pushed out.

"Davis is not the only person who understands you, Cason." Natalie wiped at her own tears. "I can get you a therapist."

"Mom, please listen to me." Cason gritted her teeth. "This is not your disease. This is not your call. And you don't even know Davis. You don't know anything about who he is."

"I won't have it. I will not have you hanging around some criminal who was just stabbed, for God's sake."

"Not your call, Mom," Cason said softly, refusing to rise to her mother's level of irritation. "I don't have a lot of say in my life, but I have say in who my friends are."

"You are going to be fine. Hanging out with these children who are so sick is not going to help you get better, Cason."

"Are you listening to yourself?" Incredulity filled her voice. "I am one of those children now."

chapter Thirteen

Davis had to go to the police department. It had been a week since his assault. He wanted to pull the covers over his head and pretend that today was not going to happen. Or better yet, that it already had. But early-May sunlight filtered into his room, and his ribs ached more than they had since the fight. All of it was a reminder that the day had started and he had to go to the police. He'd lost the game of Uno and made a promise to Cason.

Now he was up, he was moving. He'd texted Cason and found out she'd be at the clinic for most of the day getting more blood. He was going to the police because it was right thing to do. He could do one small thing. He was also doing it because it would make his parents proud. And since that day nearly a year ago, when he'd had to call them to tell them he was in jail, he would do whatever he could to earn their respect back.

Standing in the parking lot of the police station, he pulled up every ounce of courage he had and walked in. The building was sterile, with old, plastic, upholstered chairs against the walls, leaving a huge, empty space in the middle. His frantic mind wondered if criminals ever solved their problems with dance-offs in the middle. He walked to the counter where a woman was sitting and staring at a computer screen. "Can I help you?"

"I need to see Detective Avery."

"You are?"

"Davis Channing."

"One second." She motioned for him to have a seat in one of the worn chairs. The room felt empty. There was no artwork on the walls, just the same posters that were in every police station. The chairs were covered in old vinyl leather cracking from age. He could see the frayed cotton poking through it, and he had to fight not to pick at it. The sharp edges of the vinyl scratched his arm as he moved it restlessly against the armrest. He fought the dread that moved along his body like tentacles.

The taste of the Oxy filled his mouth.

Instead of making a break for it and heading to the dealer he was here to turn in, he walked calmly to the public water fountain and gulped. He splashed some of the water on his face and neck, doing anything to calm his nerves.

Why was he even here? Davis had a record, he was a known addict. Why would he think that he deserved to be helped? Nothing replaced the taste of dope, but the smell of burnt coffee and old air freshener seemed to tamp it down a little.

He picked at the chair, feeling the cotton from the busted vinyl between his fingers. He shouldn't even be here. He should be at home or work or anywhere else. He shouldn't be taking up the time of the detectives. He should just leave all of this alone.

The thoughts continued to pour over the synapses in his brain, his own lack of self-worth filling each of the empty spaces in his brain. Davis knew that it was important for him to do this, but in the same breath, he didn't think he deserved any help.

Then again, he hadn't deserved to be stabbed either.

"Davis?" Detective Avery came out. He had been at the hospital that night when Davis was brought in, and his kindness had been a nice surprise in contrast to Davis's previous experience with police officers. He guessed it was different when you were the victim versus the perpetrator. "Come on back."

There was no turning back. Davis followed the detective down a hallway to an empty room. There was a table, a couch, a trash can, and probably some surveillance equipment somewhere. Davis sat down in a hard chair across from Detective Avery. Immediately, his foot began to bounce. He didn't bother trying to stop it.

"How are you doing, Davis?" The detective smiled, but Davis was sure it wasn't real.

I shouldn't be here. The words whispered in his mind, a soft lie, tickling his receptors, and sliding into his stomach. *I deserved it.*

"Fine." Davis lied instead.

"I've seen your rap sheet." No beating around the bush. Davis didn't have anything to say, he couldn't deny it.

"It doesn't matter to me if you're still using or not, what happened to you makes you a victim."

"I'm sober." Davis defended. "I've been sober for eight months."

"And that's great, but what I'm telling you is you were assaulted, and it's my job to convict the person who did this to you."

"It was Ethan Finley." The name rushed out so easily, like he was saying who a classmate was. "Ethan's my old dealer. My ex-girlfriend got in some trouble with him and had me set up to take the blame."

"Okay." Detective Avery began to write on the yellow legal pad, the pen gliding over the paper in silence, neat rows of letters appearing. "Let's talk about Ethan and your ex-girlfriend."

~

The sun glared, hurting Davis's still-bruised head. He couldn't drive because of the head injury, so he walked the few blocks to the closest MARTA train station. The weather was perfect, sunny, with puffy clouds peeking around the skyscrapers downtown. Davis didn't know exactly how he was feeling. There was relief certainly, but it was mixed with a murkiness he didn't quite understand.

Without warning, need filled his head, taking over the pain from his concussion, and the taste of dope filled his mouth, his throat, choking him. Now his body was a prisoner to the need to use.

Just one hit.

It was a punch to his gut. As literal as the one he'd gotten from Ethan. The deep desire, the need, drove through his stomach, up into his lungs, and pooled in his mouth.

Just one hit.

The words whispered into his brain, into his heart.

chapter Fourteen

Heather wasn't there today. That left Cason playing Solitaire with actual cards instead of on an iPad. She felt positively vintage. The room was fuller, with more kids getting treatment. The kids seemed sicker. More kids were sleeping, laying in the recliners, more held by lagging parents or just gazing out the window. The patients were all ages, from babies with their blankets, pacifiers, and missing baby curls, to other teens.

Davis walked in.

Cason took a minute to stare at him unabashedly. His hair was disheveled, but that meant he probably didn't pay much attention to it. His face wasn't as swollen as it had been, but the bruises were starting to turn a deep blue instead of purple. She knew next would be green and then that sickly yellow. He was tall, and lately she thought more and more about how she fit perfectly just under his chin. Why hadn't she noticed this in all the years they'd been in school together? Why had she never paid attention to Davis Channing a day in her life?

Because her life had been buried in the dance studio doing *attitudes* and *pliés*.

"So, want to know where I was this morning?" Davis sat next to her, grinning in a full and relaxed manner.

"Is it the reason you're so off-the-charts happy?"

"Nah, that's 'cause you're here."

"You're happy because I'm in the fishbowl?" Cason didn't know how to flirt. Who knew that having cancer would be the thing that gave her a taste of normalcy?

"No, because I'm in the same place you are. That's why I'm happy." He shook his head. "And because I went to the police station this morning."

"You went to the police?"

"Yes." Cason watched his face, how relaxed it was despite the bruises and cuts, how he seemed to have a lighter appearance. "I think Officer Avery's really going to do something."

"You got the crap beaten out of you. They have to do something." She didn't feel relieved. Her pulse thickened with worry for him.

"I think they will." His grin lit up his eyes behind the ghastly bruises. "Now, onto my next problem."

"And what's that?" She raised what little was left of her eyebrows.

"You still don't think you're going to camp."

"Davis." She groaned and leaned her head back, closing her eyes. "Don't do this, please." She was not going to go to camp. It was pointless. She still didn't understand why anyone would want to go to cancer camp. Puke and discussions about what treatment you were on didn't sound like a lot of fun.

"I'm not going to pressure you." He shuffled another deck of Uno cards. Did he travel with a set now? Challenge filled his overly charming eyes. "I'll make a bet with you." He shuffled the deck. "The worst that happens? You go to camp for one week. Unless you're me, then that's the best-case scenario."

"And what's my best-case scenario?" She reached for the cards; no way was he dealing this hand.

"I'll shave my head and keep it that way the entire time you're on chemo. And," he added an incentive, "I'll never mention you going to camp again."

"The entire time?" A new vindictive glint filled her eyes. "No matter what?"

"No matter what." He smiled as she dealt the cards.

As if the electricity had been turned up and then amplified in the room, Cason felt the few hairs she had left stand up on the back of her neck. She shuffled the cards twice more before dealing them out. She watched his sincere, brown eyes and his furrowed brow as he studied the cards and then the one flipped card. Uno was really a game of luck; little actual skill was involved. She studied her own cards: one reverse and a regular wild card, no draw twos or draw fours.

"If I win but decide to go to camp, will you still shave your head?"

"Are you thinking of going to camp?" Davis smiled at

her. Her heart rate sped up, a frenetic triple beat played against her ribs, and it had absolutely nothing to do with her health and everything to do with Davis Channing and his wonky smile. Maybe spending a week at camp with him wouldn't be so bad.

"No." She said it as a matter of fact. She didn't want him to know she was considering going. Plus, she wasn't sure how she felt about him shaving his head. She liked his disheveled, I-didn't-think-about-it hair and wanted him to keep it. The baldness solidarity would be nice, but he had already paid his dues, so he should get to keep his hair.

"It's not a crappy camping–in-the–middle-of-the-woods camp, Cason." She really loved the new happiness that poured through him now. "The cabins are awesome, A/C, bathrooms and showers in the cabins. I'm also guessing the girls' bathrooms are kept cleaner than the guys'." He played a red four on her green.

Cason had no choice but to play her wild and changed the color to yellow. She listened intently as Davis described every amenity of this camp. "It's all paved, no rough paths. And everything is pretty close together so you never have to walk too far."

"Is this camp or a resort?" she joked.

"Both." He played a yellow draw two. She noted that he hadn't had to draw once. At the rate they were going, this was going to be a quick game, and she was going to be packing her bags to go to camp any minute.

"How old is everyone?" Cason was sure they would be the only ones old enough to drive.

"You can go as soon as you turn seven and until you turn eighteen. There are usually a few cabins with kids between fifteen and eighteen. If you go, I'm sure Heather will pull some strings to make sure either she's your counselor or that you're with some nice girls."

Cason studied her hand and then studied Davis. "I'm going to lose," she said, then began drawing card after card, searching for one to go on the very yellow she had picked. "What if Dr. Henderson wants to do chemo or surgery or something?"

"The one thing about camp is that the doctors are usually really great about making sure you can go." He peeked over at her hand. "You are going to lose. I have all yellows and a draw four."

"Looks like you get to keep your hair, Davis Channing."

"And you get to go to camp." He was smug, and Cason almost wanted to argue just to be contrary. But she couldn't.

"Just so you know, you could have played the whole, 'I went to the police station and reported a big ol' scary drug dealer' card, and I probably would have agreed."

"You have cancer." Davis patted her hand playfully, but instead she felt flushed all over because of his fingertips. "I went easy on you."

She laughed and took a moment to feel his hand. She turned it over in hers and let his palm rest on top of hers. She noticed that the tips of each of his fingers had calluses on them, and learned through her touch alone that Davis played the guitar or bass, or maybe some other string instrument. She'd noticed it the few times they'd held hands now, and it was something she found herself unintentionally thinking about.

"What do you play?" she asked quietly, not wanting to break the moment that had suddenly intensified between them.

"Guitar, acoustic, and not well."

"I only play the radio." She laughed.

"You can be in charge of the radio at camp."

"What?" She looked up at him, still not letting go of his hand. He was letting her control the moment. His eyes locked on hers and the energy heightened. Her fingers felt each crease and crevice of his palm.

Her breath stuttered in her chest.

"At night, after evening activity, we all gather outside one of the girls' cabins and listen to music and talk and stuff." His voice sounded thicker to her.

"What else do y'all do at night?" Or maybe it was hers.

"Each night has a theme, and usually the camp is either split up or we have two different activities so the littles can get to bed."

"Littles?" She stopped playing with his hand and let her hand rest, but then her breath faltered as he began to feel each line on her palm.

"The baby campers. It's a long day and they go to bed before the older kids." He gently caressed the bruise on the top of her hand from the blood draw that morning.

"I told you about the carnival and the dance, but there's usually a movie on the ball field, and one night, a huge game of Capture the Flag."

"I would ruin anyone's chance at winning Capture the Flag."

"Mari is way too invested in it, she's probably already thinking about the best position for you. They have these huge treehouses that wheelchairs and stuff can get up to. You can see all of camp from the top and the kids who can't run or need help sit up in the tree and use these awesome walkie-talkies to tell the ground crews where stuff is and stuff like that."

Cason didn't have much else to ask. Davis kept holding her hand, skimming his thumb over the sensitive skin on the underside of her wrist. She let her head lean back and her eyes drift for a minute. Pre-meds for the blood transfusion and the excitement of the day began to catch up with her.

"You don't have to fight sleep just because Davis is here, Cason. I don't think he's going anywhere," Heather smirked as she dropped some DVDs on her way by.

Davis gripped her hand tighter before he put in one of the DVDs. Her eyes opened for a minute as he spread a blanket over her, then settled into the chair next to her.

He pressed a kiss to the top of her hand. Cason's smile was slow and her eyes slid shut.

It would do for now.

chapter Fifteen

Davis had three weeks of his junior year left, and it was getting harder to focus on AP prep tests and finals when it seemed like his mind was drifting to Cason and the hospital more and more. Since his assault, the school agreed that he only had to come for his AP classes. It was a good setup. But, today he didn't want to sit at home. And his mom had come to the rescue with an offer to take him with her to the hospital while she led the parents group.

Davis had felt annoyed most of the day, unable to drive, his head still throbbing just under his skull. But maybe going to the hospital would distract him.

"Cason's in room seven." Heather handed him an iPad and kept on walking. It was all the direction he needed. Winding down the hall, past the nurses' station and the fishbowl, he knocked on the door.

"Come in."

Davis opened the door, and her smile washed away his irritation.

"I didn't think you worked today." She was hooked up to an IV. The phlegm-y looking bag hanging next to the bed told Davis that she was getting a platelet transfusion.

"I'm not actually working." There was just a moment of pretense where he debated about where to sit in the room, then he climbed into the bed, moving IV tubing and things. If he got in trouble, he'd just blame his concussion. No nurse would be mad at him when he had a head injury. Maybe it was the impulsivity of said head injury, but he laced his fingers through Cason's, feeling the way their palms met, their fingers gripped.

Cason's smile grew and a deep flush filled her cheeks, a splotch of red on her neck, just below the hollow of her throat. But, she didn't pull away or seem put off. She squeezed his fingers before laying her head back against the small pillow. "I'm glad you're not actually working."

"My mom is leading the parents group and I couldn't focus at school." He could feel the little pricks from her shaved head against his cheek, her warm breath against his neck.

"Which is probably why mine had to run to a very important meeting," Cason laughed.

"I didn't even ask how your immune system was doing," Davis commented on their proximity. "Do I need to move?"

"My white cells are climbing and hemoglobin is okay, but my platelets were too low," Cason explained.

They were both quiet, but the air was heavy with all the unspoken words between them. Davis circled his thumb on the outside of her hand, over the spot that he had kissed just last week. "Whatcha thinking about?" He could feel the itchiness receding, like he'd been given something for an allergy. Just being here, with her, seemed to be the balm he needed.

"It's stupid." She didn't look at him, instead turning her head farther into his shoulder.

"No it's not."

"I've been thinking about camp." Her voice was muffled against his shirt, her breath hot through the cotton. "And the dance."

"Oh." Davis slid his arm around her, tucking her into his body with her IV tubing resting between them, the constant reminder that Cason was actually in the hospital. "What about the dance?"

"You'll think it's stupid." She still wouldn't look at him, but he could hear the way her voice had thickened. This was real, whatever it was.

"I will never think anything you say is stupid." He wanted to pull her tighter, but they were already breaking all sorts of rules. Rules that probably could get him fired from his volunteer position.

She still didn't look up at him. Davis could barely make out the curve of her cheek, her nose, and her soft lips as they pressed against him. "I wanted to dance with you." Cason's words were muted against him. "I wanted to dance, and it bothered me that I'll never dance with you the way I could have."

Davis was quiet for minute, letting her words sink in,

tumble around his brain for a bit, and then he repeated them in his mind.

Cason wanted to dance.

With him.

Reaching with his other hand, he got the iPad Heather had given him. This was either going to be great, or going to end all chances he had with her.

He slid off the bed and stood, holding his hand out to her. "Then dance with me."

"Davis," she groaned, but he could hear the sadness just under her voice.

Maybe he could be her balm now.

"It's not the camp dance, but we'll get to dance there later this summer. This is just preparation." He flipped the overhead light off, allowing only the early spring sun to shine through the blinds in the room. It wasn't like there was a lot of room, they wouldn't be able to do more than sway together, but this wasn't a movie musical. They only needed the sounds of music to cover the busyness of the clinic outside.

Cason gingerly took his hand and let him help her balance in his arms. She couldn't put weight on the leg that was in the brace, so it was up to him to keep her standing.

Davis straightened the IV tubing again, making sure she wasn't going to accidentally de-access her port and send platelets dripping out onto the floor.

He gently wrapped his arms around her waist, bringing her lithe body in line with his, holding her close. He could feel each beat of her heart on his chest and her soft breath against the hollow of his throat. He tightened his hold, wanting to hold tighter to her, to this moment.

"I had no idea." Cason whispered the words against him.

"What?" he asked against the shell of her ear. He could feel her small hands around his neck, just fingering the short hair there, drawing little lines and designs into it.

"I didn't know I'd miss this." She pulled back just a little, and he tightened his grip to make sure she was stable. "I knew I'd miss ballet, I knew I'd have to stop dancing for a while. But I didn't know that I had also decided I'd never dance at all again."

"Cason, do you remember ever not dancing?" Davis traced his thumb over her cheek, resting just behind her ear.

"No," she smiled. "It's my earliest memory."

"Then I have no doubt that you will be back dancing in those ballet shoes."

She coughed over the words, changing the subject. Cason lightly traced the scar just under his chin. "What's this from?"

"Scar from my last surgery. The lymphoma had spread more than they thought initially, and they had to remove some of my lymph nodes there." They weren't moving anymore, not even pretending to dance, but his arms were still wrapped tightly around her waist. Cason traced the scar once more with the softest touch, and then gently traced the dimple beside his mouth. "Because of the surgery, my smile went off."

"Your smile is one of my favorite things." Cason's voice was hot on his skin. "And not just on you, like, it's one of my favorite things in this world."

"I say I have a smile with a wink." He wanted to smile bigger, to give her the full effect of his all-on-one-side-of-his-face smile, but couldn't. Cason was too close, her breath stealing all his rational thoughts about immune systems and why he most definitely shouldn't kiss her.

He kissed her anyway.

It was just barely a kiss, their lips just touching, their breaths held.

"Cason? I need— Oh!" Heather didn't knock. Or if she had, Davis hadn't heard. They couldn't pull apart too fast, he had to make sure Cason was going to be able to stand. And this just prolonged the embarrassment and let Heather revel in all the discomfort. "Huh. Everything okay?"

Davis was absolutely positive he had never felt this level of embarrassment in his entire life. And he'd done some really stupid things, but none of it compared to this humiliation that fired through his veins. "Yep. Everything's good."

"Cason, let's get you back in bed." Heather pushed Davis aside and she got Cason settled again. "Your platelets are almost done. I'm going to go get your nurse, but I am leaving this door open!"

Davis nodded with as much contriteness as he could and watched as Heather left. He had only just reached for Cason's hand when Heather came back in, swiping the iPad and marching back out. "I am never going to hear the end of this." He let his head fall on the side of the bed, looking at the floor through the crack. "She is going to hound me for the rest of my life."

"At least it wasn't my mom." Cason patted the back of his head before letting her hand rest there.

"Thank God for small mercies." Davis laughed. It was a good laugh, breaking the tension that had filled the room with Heather's entrance.

"A smile with a wink, huh?" Cason touched his scar once again. "I like it."

"Thanks." His face was still burning with heat, but seemed to be calming a little.

"I like you." She chewed on her lip, the only sign of her insecurity.

"We'll let it be our secret." He smiled and kissed her hand on the center of her palm, closing her fingers around it.

~

Not long after, Natalie came back from lunch and Davis had to find something else to do. He sat in Heather's office, helping her sort the new patient information folders and doing his best to keep Heather from interrogating him about what she'd walked in on.

"Hey, Heather, can I borrow Davis?" One of the nurse practitioners popped her head in. "Jared is here and having a hard time calming down today."

"Sure thing," Davis jumped in before Heather could stop him. He knew he was still recovering, the constant hum of pain in his head wouldn't let him forget. He stood slowly, feeling a pull on his wound. "Where is he?"

"Over in the procedure room."

The procedure room was between the fishbowl and the waiting room. It was a place where kids could be sedated for procedures in the clinic, like bone marrow biopsies and spinal taps. Davis knew from talking with Jared's grandmother that he had relapsed.

This relapse meant Jared would probably be transferring to hospice care soon.

But right now, Jared was there and needed to be distracted.

"Hey, man," Davis wished the lights had been dimmed so maybe the spots would stop dancing. He wasn't sure what was causing the headache right now: impending migraine or concussion. "What's up?"

Davis did his best to distract Jared while the nurses and docs got set up for his procedure. They were going to be testing his bone marrow to see how many leukemia cells were present, how far his disease had progressed.

It wasn't easy to get Jared to refocus, but Davis managed to get him interested in playing a game of Slaps with the cards. He wasn't letting the kid win, but Davis could see Jared's delayed reaction to things.

A cheer of victory resounded as Jared took the last of Davis's cards.

"We're ready." One of the nurses smiled at Jared and held the door open for Davis.

"I'll see you in a bit." Davis gave him a manly hug instead of what he wanted to do, which was hold on to him for a bit. This whole situation was shitty.

He walked outside the procedure room, away from Jared and the nurses. He leaned back against the wall and took a few deep breaths. Knowing that Jared had relapsed, and seeing he was just the same eleven-year-old punk, made the whole thing so much worse. And real.

He looked up from the tile floor to see a procedure tray that contained not only needles and antiseptic, but, several fentanyl patches.

Easy.

Before Davis could think through what was happening, he watched as his hands started to reach toward the tray.

It'd be so easy to take them.

Just do it.

One more time.

Excuse after excuse to make it acceptable filled his brain. The words were so loud, screaming, taking up all the space for anything else.

He couldn't get away.

Just once.

Like he was watching a movie, he saw his hand slam back away from the tray. He pushed off the wall, practically running from the offending tray. From the desire. From his past. From Ethan.

Moron.

His brain screamed obscenities and Davis just ran.

He ran down the stairs to the basement of the hospital where his mom would be.

"Davis?" Amanda came out of the conference room, concern reflected in her eyes.

"Maybe this was too much." He couldn't tell her the truth. He couldn't tell his mom that he'd nearly stolen a patch meant to relieve Jared of the pain from dying of cancer.

"I'm done. Let's get you home." She put an arm around him, holding him close, still protecting her son. Relief flooded him with the comforting scent his mom had: fresh laundry and freesia.

"Thanks, Mom." And he meant it. His mom was saving him again.

~

"Do you want me to come with you?" Amanda sat in the driver's seat outside the church where his NA meeting was. "I can."

"I'm good." Davis ran a hand over his hair, pulling it

back just far enough to feel the painful tug. "I'll text when we're getting ready to finish."

"Sounds great."

Davis got out of the car and watched as his mom drove off. He hadn't been to a meeting since his assault, and hadn't planned on coming tonight, but his reaction to the drugs, the painful pull that had filled his body, reminded him that he was an addict. He needed this system to aid in his recovery.

Sitting down on the steps, he put his head in his hands. He needed a moment to himself, a moment to collect his thoughts before he went into the meeting. A sizable part of him wished he smoked like many others who were in recovery did. Then he might have something to calm his shaking hands and twittering nerves.

The sounds of someone walking up the steps caused Davis to look up. And like a dream, a bad one, he saw Alexis walking slowly toward him. He should have gone to another meeting place. He shouldn't have kept to his routine.

"Hey." Alexis sat next to him.

"I think you're in the wrong place." Acid churned in his stomach and the still-healing stitches pulled as he moved. His adrenaline was pulsing so hard and fast in his veins, he could feel it moving in his skull. Or are you for real this time and want to get some help?" He tried not to think about the last time he invited her to a meeting.

"Why don't you come with me instead, you can stop running, stop the *ache*," she purred, tracing a finger down his chest. He wanted to throw up. Because he did want to go with her, desperately. He wouldn't be in danger anymore once Ethan realized he was getting one of his prime clients back. And yes . . . the ache.

Seeing Alexis twisted his stomach, and a hot balloon of need dragged at him.

He could blow off the meeting, he could walk down the steps with the person who'd gotten him stabbed, just so he could score.

"No thanks." The words burned his tongue. Alexis pushed her body into his, and her stringy, dirty curls brushed his nose and chin. All he could smell was smoke and dope. His brain fired, and a cold sweat slid down his back.

"Ethan wanted to know if you had his stuff." She stopped trying to flirt with him, to get him to come with her. She was all business now.

Just one more.

"The only thing I have for Ethan is a TPO and a warrant for his arrest." Davis wanted to run away, but made himself stand and walk slowly up the steps, toward his NA meeting. Good intentions and guilt stopped him.

"You created this. You owe me, you know."

"I paid any debt I owe you." He ripped her hand from his arm and went into the church.

He didn't look back.

"Hey, you okay?" John was freshening up the coffee for the meeting.

"Alexis Foster." He didn't have to elaborate. This was one of those instances where it was helpful that John was not only his sponsor but his school counselor. He knew exactly who Alexis was.

"Why don't we grab a coffee after the meeting?"

"Sure." Davis blew out a breath. "Can you give me a ride home? I told Mom I'd text her, but if you could save her the trip . . ." Davis felt only mildly sheepish about asking. "After concussions, they don't like you driving."

"Yeah." John put a reassuring hand on Davis's shoulder and walked him to the seats. "It'll be like old times."

The meeting chairman called the meeting to order. It was a path Davis knew well by now, something he could coast through without paying attention. His head was aching and his ribs were sore. He could still smell Alexis, and if he tried hard enough, he could recall the way she used to smell. She used to have a soft fragrance, something like cotton, but then it had all been covered by the stench of hopelessness.

He didn't realize that he'd moved until he felt the wood of the podium under his hands.

"I'm Davis and I'm an addict." He began his story.

chapter sixteen

"Mom!" Cason called out of the bathroom. "Can you help me?" She sat by the tub as the water was heating up. She hated that she couldn't do this on her own. She felt like a child being watched to make sure she didn't drown. But she hadn't quite learned how to navigate getting in and out yet. Her leg was so fragile that one wrong move and any healing would be undone.

"What's up?" Her mom appeared, completely dressed and ready to leave. "I have to be out of here in ten minutes."

"Crap, the board meeting."

"Yeah, they moved it for me." It was usually held in early April, but it had been moved to later in May to help out. Natalie helped Cason stand, before closing the Velcro around her brace. "I promise I'll help you this afternoon when I get back."

Cason tried not to pout. She was so tired of wearing the brace, the way it wrapped up around her leg, confining her. She wanted to be able to shower on her own terms, not when her mom had the half hour to help her. "It's fine." Once she was strapped back in and re-dressed, she followed her mom to her room.

"You're not dirtier than after a dance rehearsal, so waiting a few more hours won't hurt you." Her mom paced the room, picking up earrings, deeming them not right, putting them down, trying another pair. She was worried. Cason could see it in the tightness around her lips and the rigidity of her posture. "But if it's really bothering you, I can reschedule this meeting."

"Mom, you can't reschedule a meeting with the board. They're your boss." Cason sighed and sat her magazine back down. "I'll be fine."

"You're sure you're okay?"

"My counts are good. I feel good today." Cason motioned to the mound of magazines and books she had spread around her. "I'm just going to read and lounge." There wasn't anything else she could do.

"Why don't I bring you some snacks for while I'm gone? That way you won't have to get up."

"Mom, you've never been overprotective a day in my life. Let's not start now." Frustration filled her voice.

Her mom sat beside her on the bed. "I know." Natalie pursed her lips, really looking at her.

"I'll be fine, don't keep the board waiting."

She took a sip of her Coke and watched as her mother hurried out the door. She flipped through magazines, texted Davis, got emails from Mari, and watched *Chopped* on Food Network. She responded to the emails, sent Davis more texts, and was thoroughly bored.

Cason was seventeen. She could take care of herself.

She needed a shower and was tired of having to wait on her mommy to come and help her. She reasoned that she'd been showering independently for as long as she could remember. She could do it now.

Rising from her bed, she slowly made her way to the bathroom. She hung her towels, turned the water on, and debated the best way to get herself into the tub. The sliding shower door made it difficult to sit and swing her legs over. She knew better than to try and put any weight on her leg, so she'd have to use her crutches. There was a chair for her to sit in once she actually got in the tub.

It would be fine.

It would be perfect.

She could do this. Gingerly, she made her way into the tub and let the spray hit her. She didn't think she'd felt this good about something since she'd completed a set of *fouettés* for the first time. Showering was so underrated, especially when it was no longer a daily occurrence. She didn't have hair to wash anymore, but being clean and getting out of her brace for a short period of time was nice.

It was all perfect.

Until it wasn't.

chapter seventeen

Davis was bussing a table for the umpteenth time that morning. College students filled every table, studying for finals. The jingle of the door let him know he needed to get back behind the counter. Mark, the regular who had been dealing with hard times since losing his job, came in. He looked better than he had in a while.

"Morning." Davis greeted cheerily.

"Hey there." Mark smiled and it finally went all the way to his eyes. "Coffee and a bagel." Davis served him, watching as he slid his card through the card reader and signed. Mark walked out the door, a swing in his step. When Davis turned the card reader back around, he saw that Mark had tipped him the exact amount of the bagel and coffee he'd given him weeks ago. It was a nice feeling, knowing that he'd helped someone.

Davis served patrons and texted Cason between jobs. He knew she was bored out of her mind right now. He also knew that if he'd switched shifts to hang out with her, she'd be offended. She'd told him as much when he'd offered to let her come hang at his place while he worked. He doubted Mrs. Martin would want them home alone together.

"Davis?" Ike, his manager, called over the counter. "Phone."

Davis walked across the café, taking the phone from him. "Hello?"

"Hey." He'd recognize that voice anywhere. "It's me."

"Alexis." Of course she didn't call his cellphone. He wouldn't have answered it.

"I'm sorry about everything." He could hear the tears in her voice. "Davis, I need you to come through for me." She was weepy, which told Davis she was coming down from a binge.

"Alexis." He shouldn't engage her in any way, but there he was. He still wanted to help her. "I can't do this. I can't score anything for you. Let me help. I can call Mr. Williams. Get you into treatment."

"I don't know." She sniffled. "I'm so sorry." She was full on crying now.

"I can't talk to you if you're not willing to get help."

"Bye, Davis." Alexis hung up before he could even find out where she was. He hated that what he felt was relief. Then, before he'd even gotten the phone back in its cradle, his own phone rang.

"Cason." Talking to Cason would get rid of the irritation that Alexis left behind.

"Uh, Davis?" It was Natalie. She sounded upset. "We're at the hospital."

"What?" His heart stopped. "What's wrong?"

"Cason fell in the shower." He could hear the edge of

hysteria in her voice, this was definitely bad. Definitely not what they wanted to have happen. "She's in CT right now. She asked for you."

"I'm on my way." First, heat had filled his stomach, and then immediately, it cooled. He had forgotten Alexis, and all he could think of was his girlfriend. "It's Cason," he said to Ike.

"It's good." Ike smiled, attempting to reassure him. "I've got it covered."

"Are you sure?" Davis didn't want to leave Ike short-handed, but he wanted to be with Cason, to make sure she was fine. Just to make sure.

"Yes." Ike practically shoved him out the door. "Go to your girl."

~

Davis chewed off every fingernail he had left while he waited for Cason to get back from CT. Heather stopped by, bringing hospital coffee to him and Mrs. Martin. Cason had been in radiology for what felt like forever.

"Is she okay?" He stared at his coffee as he spoke to Natalie. Guilt washed over him. He knew he should have called out of work to stay with her.

"She was in enormous pain." Natalie was disheveled, her blond hair falling out of some complicated twist. Dark circles shadowed her eyes. She seemed to have aged in the twelve hours since Davis had last seen her. "She fell in the shower. She somehow managed to get out of the shower after falling, but God knows how." Natalie sniffed hard, clenching a used tissue. "She didn't want to call me because I was at a meeting, but there was swelling."

"What happened? Did she call you?" Davis asked.

"She called the hospital." Natalie laughed over the tears that slid down her face. "She talked to her nurse and they paged Dr. Henderson. I actually met the ambulance at the door." Something about this part of the story seemed to break Natalie. "She's just a kid. She shouldn't know how to have her oncologist paged."

It was the only time Davis had ever seen Natalie Martin openly weep.

The surgeon walked in. "Dr. Lee," Natalie said. Davis didn't know proper protocol. Should he leave? Should he stay and be supportive of Mrs. Martin? "How's Cason?"

"Resting." Dr. Lee smiled softly. "Davis, why don't you go see her? I'm sure a friendly face would be nice." As he left, he heard the surgeon say, "I'm afraid we're going to need to take Cason into surgery later today."

This was not good.

"Hey, you," he said, entering Cason's room, and had to mentally remind himself to walk instead of run to her side so he didn't startle her. She looked terrible. Her face was drawn, tears stained her hollow cheeks, and she had dark circles under her eyes. Her lips were chapped and gray. She almost looked like a black-and-white photo.

"Hey." She sniffled and wiped at her cheeks with a well-worn tissue.

"What happened?" He wanted to crawl into the bed with her, to hold her close to him, to feel her heart beating, but he knew that he'd just get in trouble. Instead, he took her hand and held it in his hand, a thumb running over her knuckles.

"I fell." She sniffed again. "I was just so tired of waiting on everyone to help me." He could see anger glittering behind unshed tears. "I just wanted to shower. Isn't that stupid?"

"No," he reassured her. "It was an accident, Cason."

"An accident that makes it impossible to do a limb salvage. I have to have an . . ." The words seemed frozen in her throat, but he knew what they were. "They're going to amputate."

Davis felt his breath stick in his chest. "Why?"

"Turns out my leg is broken in pieces. Dr. Lee said the surgery needed to be soon because of vascular issues." Davis could hear the tears clogging her throat and coating the words as she spoke. " 'Mush' is the word Dr. Lee used."

"What does this mean?"

"You can't fix mush." The tears were harder, real sobs coming from her. "They're going to try to save as much of my leg as they can."

Fuck it. He climbed into the bed, holding her close and letting her sob out her sadness and grief. His own heart crumbled out of him and onto the hard, tiled floor of the hospital.

"I just wanted to be the one to make the decision."

She gripped him, holding onto him like he was keeping her from drowning. "I wanted to be able to make the call, like with my hair. It felt so good, and I needed that again."

"I know." He held her tight, like he was trying to pull her sadness into himself. "I know you did."

"It's not fair. None of it is fair."

"It's not." He agreed. He didn't have words of comfort for this, nothing he'd learned in NA or his own private therapy sessions had prepared him for a girlfriend who was going to lose her leg. This was grief of its own kind.

"I was one of the best damn dancers in the nation. I was brilliant."

"I know." He had spent so much time high and never noticed Cason before she got sick. Now he wished he could have seen her dance in person, watched her glide across the stage and fling herself through the air.

"I had great feet and turnout that made others jealous." He didn't know what any of that meant, but it sounded impressive to him. "I hate this."

"You should," he agreed. He didn't want to tell her any of the stupid comforting words that others were going to tell her. This was not fair. This was a nightmare. And it was Cason's real life. Later today, surgeons would work to save what they could of her leg, the leg that only months ago had been perfect and healthy and had moved her around in a beautiful way. The muscles and bone that had once allowed her to balance on only her toes were now mush.

~

The clock on the wall was broken. Davis looked at it for the fifth time in ten minutes and determined it was starting to go backward. That had to be the reason that it had only been an hour since they had taken Cason into surgery. He checked his phone to be sure that he'd read it right and was frustrated to find that the clock was wrong, and it hadn't even been an hour yet. Cason might not even be in surgery yet, still waiting for it to start, and sound asleep. He'd stayed with her until Natalie had arrived, then left to give them some privacy. Now he swirled his coffee, offered to run and get more for anyone else in the surgical waiting area, and checked his email, repeatedly. Five new emails waited for him, all saying the same thing.

```
From: A. Foster

To: D. Channing

Subject: I'm sorry

I'm sorry.

I can't be helped.

Live a good life.

—A
```

He didn't know what it meant. Alexis might need him for something, but his brain could only process one trauma at a time and Cason took precedence.

Just one hit.

His brain begged and pleaded for relief from his stress.

"Davis, I'll text you when the doctors update." Heather said. "Why don't you go outside? Get some air."

"You sure? I could go get more coffee or snacks."

"If we have any more coffee, we're going to be up for days," she said. "I'll sit with Natalie. You take care of Davis for a bit."

He hugged her and made his way to the gardens outside the hospital. The old, pebbled paths were familiar and reminded him of his days on chemo. His mind replayed the conversation with Cason over again. Had it only been the day before that he'd danced with her? That he'd kissed her?

Just one more hit.

That would make the ache in his chest disappear.

The taste of an indescribable high filled his mouth and nose. He could feel the straw and tinfoil in his hand and smell the acrid scent of chemicals burning. His palms shook and his lungs tightened at the thought of just one hit. Just one to ease this horrible discomfort in his chest. He wanted it desperately. He wanted to let the void fill his head and erase these feelings. He didn't want to feel right now, it all hurt in a way he didn't understand, and he wanted to fix it.

A quick high would fix all of it.

Davis sat down hard in the middle of the path, thankful that no one was around to watch as he began to shake. His palms were sweating. He dropped his head between his knees, his forehead nearly touching the pavement below.

Deep breaths, he commanded himself. Deep breaths, clean air. Fresh air. Oxygen.

In. Out.

In. Out.

In. Out.

His stomach churned as his body fought itself. He felt as nauseated as he had on chemo, as he had in withdrawals. He gagged and fought not to throw up.

With shaking hands, he pulled his phone from his pocket and pressed blindly at it, moving it to his ear in jerky motions.

"I want to use." He breathed roughly. "I know where to get it, and I want to."

"Where are you?" John answered swiftly.

"Hospital garden." He gagged again and spit on the ground, hoping to rid his mouth of the taste. "Cason is in surgery. I can't fix this."

But his mind screamed that he could.

Just one more hit.

Tears ran down his cheeks, and he didn't even bother to wipe them away.

chapter eighteen

She was frozen, her arms lifted over her head, perfectly still. A lesser dancer would be shaking with the strain of the position, but not Cason. Right now, she could hold this forever. Nothing hurt. Lightning shocks slid through her muscles, tightening each one in her arms, fingers, and legs as she prepared for her cue.

She shivered as nausea and nerves filled her stomach. Her hair was pulled back tight from her face and sprayed down. A bright spotlight lit her body. The momentary heat filled her and then disappeared, her nerves taking over. Then there was her cue: the music swelled and she broke the pose, moving into the dance.

She spun, her toes tightly held in her satin pointe shoes. They were perfectly broken in and the typical ache of pressure was gone.

She was flying. Her leaps had never been more effortless, more perfect.

God, this was pure magic.

Confident in her movements, she danced in tight circles around the vacant stage, gliding. Her *pirouettes* were pristine.

Floating.

Again.

How was she actually floating?

"Cason?" A light burned into her eyes, too bright. Too white. It all hurt her head. She was shaking with cold. "It's over. You did beautifully."

"My dance?" She croaked, her throat hurt. *Why did everything hurt?*

"The surgery." Dr. Lee's face came into focus. Her eyes, soft, kind, and maybe a bit sad.

Cason's brain cleared instantly. The pain became more forceful, filling her veins, tightening her muscles. Her limbs were so heavy, but she moved a hand over her body. The brace was gone. The constant companion of so many months, gone.

"You've got on a fishnet stocking of sorts. It's holding the dressing around your surgical site," Dr. Lee explained. Tubes and wires pulled at her skin, but she still moved her hand down.

Over the fishnets.

And then nothing.

Her leg was gone.

There was nothing there.

Just a rounded end covered in gauze and packing.

There were no pirouettes, no leaps, no pointe shoes.

Nothing.

"Cason." It was her mother. *Where had she come from?* "How are you, baby?" Natalie spoke to her like a child, not like her former star ballerina. Not like the protégé she had been.

"It's gone, Mama." The words were thick and stuck in her mouth. They hurt to speak. "My leg."

"Cason, we're giving you some more sedative." Dr. Lee sounded so far away. "You need to rest."

It hurt. Everything hurt. A nasal cannula was slipped around her face. She tried to swipe it away, but her remaining limbs were weighed down. Sadness held her heart and soul in claws that were digging into her beaten body. She fought not to scream, not to scratch and hit at the tangible demons tearing at her.

Without consent, her brain clouded and slid into the off position.

Nothing hurt.

But everything did.

chapter nineteen

"Davis." Mr. Williams sat with him at a small table at the Daily Grind. "How are you doing?" Two days ago, Mr. Williams had practically scraped him off the hospital garden's path. He had been so broken, desperate to use in those hours of Cason's amputation.

"Okay." He couldn't spend every waking moment with her at the hospital. Dr. H had kicked him out and reminded him that he had a life outside of Cason.

"Really?" The words were filled with disbelief. "Have you seen Cason?"

"I've stopped by, but she's still pretty out of it. They're having a hard time getting her pain under control."

"How does that make you feel?"

"Worried more than anything else." Davis flattened out his straw against the tabletop. "I'm not worried about her becoming an addict or anything, I'm worried about how she's going to live with one leg."

"She'll adapt, Davis. Have faith in her."

Davis nodded, but there was a part of him that wasn't completely sure that Cason would adapt. Her whole world had been tied to the five toes and bones of that leg.

Mr. Williams's phone vibrated on the table, startling them both as it broke the silence. "Let me get this," he apologized as he answered.

Davis didn't listen, he flattened the straw more and then began to twist it around his finger, wrapping it up and letting it unravel.

The air changed, and that should have clued Davis in. He should have realized right then that something had changed, something had happened. Mr. Williams turned away, looking out the café window, but Davis watched the lines around his eyes deepen, then he gave a deep sigh as he spoke.

This was all bad.

"Davis?" Mr. Williams's tone changed, his voice completely different than it had been just a moment before. He sat the offending phone down between them, the face still bright from the call. "Alexis OD'd." His eyes held a somberness, and the wrinkles around his eyes were deeper. His mouth was tight in a straight line.

"What?" Davis wasn't sure he had heard Mr. Williams correctly.

"That was the school letting me know that she had OD'd." Mr. Williams spoke in his best school counselor voice, but it did nothing to calm the firestorm working through Davis's blood, the anxiety that didn't bother to creep, but skittered over all his synapses.

"Did she get naloxone?" Davis asked about the meds that could keep an overdose from killing a person.

"No, her parents found her this morning." Mr. Williams leveled his kindest eyes at Davis, letting him know that this was serious, that Davis needed to hear the truth in his words. "She's gone."

Davis let those words move through his thoughts, let them roll in the cracks and fissures in his mind. The sentence didn't seem to be able to penetrate through the thick film covering his brain, instead the whole sentence just slid along, making him repeat them over and over and over.

Alexis is gone. Alexis OD'd. Alexis is gone.

All the air in Davis's body stopped circulating. And when it restarted, his heart tittered and then began pounding in such a ferocious beat that all he could hear was blood pumping.

Mr. Williams said something about it not being his fault, but Davis didn't really hear him. He tried to remember the email. He tried to remember the words from when she called. But Cason had eclipsed all of it. And in the end, it had been Alexis who was dying.

"I should have done something." His voice was harsh, full of anguish.

"Davis, listen to me." John made Davis meet his eyes. "You cannot help everyone. You can only help yourself. You can't control other people and what they do."

"Yeah, I know."

"You control how you choose to deal with it," Mr. Williams reminded him. "You are admitting that you can't change what happened or what will happen, but you are taking control of what is going on right now."

His soul felt so empty.

His brain begged for a moment of quiet.

And dear God, he wanted to use.

chapter Twenty

"How are you feeling?" Heather asked from the rocking chair near her bed. Cason noticed her long hair had been twisted up into some intricate knot that probably only took seconds to accomplish but looked like it took hours. She also noticed that Heather looked tired. She rarely looked tired, but she did right now. Must be a lot going on.

Cason stared straight ahead. She'd been in the hospital for four days.

She no longer had a left leg. Instead, she had a residual limb that was about half of her thigh, maybe a little longer. Dr. Lee assured her that it was a good amount considering how high her tumor had started. She wasn't in pain, but she wasn't sure if she was actually feeling anything. She tried to find something to be upset about, to feel something, but nothing was there.

"I'm numb."

"Numb?"

"Yeah." She picked at the blanket covering what was left of her body. "Rationally, I know this is what had to happen. Dr. Lee explained that once they got my leg open that there was very little else they could have done."

"You had a nasty tumor," Heather said, "but you knew that."

"It ate my leg." She blew out a breath. "My body went crazy and ate itself." If there had been an ounce of hysteria in her words then it probably would have sounded normal, but there wasn't.

"How's physical therapy going?" Cason knew that Heather was trying to get her to focus on something else. But all she thought about was how she didn't feel anything. She should feel something. Phantom pains, pain in general, something. And she felt nothing.

"Fine." She puffed a breath. "I stand. I practice with my crutches. I walk up and down stairs. Sometimes if I'm feeling wild, they let me use one of the fitness balls."

"Be careful, you still have staples in your residual limb. You have to heal."

Her numbness shifted, began to sting. "It isn't even over though. My diseased leg has been sawed off. But there could still be some rogue cancer in my body. I have months of chemo before I'll even know if it's really gone. Then what? Dance again? Oh wait, that's only for two-legged people." Finally, emotion clipped her words. Something was there—anger she supposed. Or exhaustion. Cason was so tired, so over her life and the path it had taken.

"This'll go by quickly." Heather took Cason's hand. "By the time camp gets here at the end of summer, you'll be back in the groove. You'll be on a prosthesis hopefully, and will be working your way toward walking. Camp has a way of offering a comfort that hospitals never can."

Camp.

Cason had no desire whatsoever to go to camp now. She didn't want to do anything. She wanted to get into PT and get a leg and get on with her life. Spending a week at camp was not in her plans. She knew she couldn't let people down, though. Even her mom had turned around about camp now that dancing was out. Natalie seemed almost like *she* wanted to go.

"You sound like Davis." Cason tried to sound less bitter than she felt, but then decided she didn't care. "He's always so optimistic about everything."

"I'll never admit it, but he's sort of smart." Heather said.

"I suppose. It's only a little annoying." It was very annoying.

"Cason, part of what you're feeling is the pain meds, but the bigger part is shock." Heather moved closer then and made Cason look at her. "You woke up one morning with a plan, you took a shower, something we all do, a basic necessity, and then you went to bed with one leg. That's a lot to process and to figure out."

"I'm not in shock," Cason rebuffed. "I always knew that could happen."

"Do I need Uno cards to get you to talk this out?"

Cason thought that was the absolute worst idea of all time. She wanted to pull the covers over her head and sleep until all of this was over. She wanted to hide in a dark room and wait for her life to resemble what it had been. She knew that it wasn't a choice. But that didn't mean she didn't long for it. Darkness would be much easier.

When she slept, she danced.

"Maybe," she said instead of all the thoughts running around in her chaotic brain. When she tried to offer a feeble smile, she felt it fall, and instead, tears flooded her eyes again. She was so sick of crying.

So sick of being sick.

Heather pulled her close, tucking her into a comfortable hug and letting Cason drip tears all over her T-shirt. She didn't cry the deep sobs of grief she had before the amputation, instead it was a slow, frustrating trickle. She wished she could cry and cry and cry until she felt better, but it wasn't there. Nothing was there. Heather didn't offer platitudes or assurances that it would get better. They both knew that this moment just sucked.

"Hey." Mari, all wild curls and sympathetic eyes, came in as Heather got up to leave. "Sorry I didn't call."

"I'm not going anywhere." Cason wiped her eyes with the scratchy hospital-grade tissues.

"Bad day?" Mari sat on the bed, like she'd been invited and was welcome.

"It's fine." She closed her eyes, not really wanting to see healthy Mari and her very prominent missing leg.

"Tell me what you're most afraid of right now."

"What?" Cason's new brows came together.

"When they did my surgery, I was terrified of them removing the drain, you know that tube that's left in you to collect residual blood. I knew from other surgeries that it was going to hurt and it's what scared me."

"Mari, really?" Cason felt hot tears filling her throat again. She didn't want to talk about any of this.

"You will dance again." Mari gripped her hands tightly. "You have to decide to do it." Cason nodded, mostly because she didn't want to let her new friend down. But she didn't really believe her.

"This is shitty, Cason." Mari's words were rough, with a little venom just underneath. "I remember it and thinking that everything was over now." Mari pushed at her dark curls and sniffed hard against her own tears. "We all have those moments." Another hard sniff, refusing to cry. "You have one leg now, but you're not less of a person."

Cason thought she was exactly one-fourth less of a person. "I'm not very good company." She wouldn't look at her friend. "I'm sorry."

Mari offered a wonky smile and wiped her tears. "You don't have to be. Why don't we watch that trashy soap?" She laughed bitterly. "That one girl is having a much worse week than we are. She's being buried alive. Again."

It sounded like the girl being buried alive might be the only one who could actually understand how Cason felt.

chapter Twenty-one

Waking up every morning to the deep, raw thirst for a high hurt more than any tumor or surgery ever had. Davis moved slowly, his ribs still bruised, his stitches finally removed, but the skin still so newly healed that it itched and burned with each movement.

And if he could just get high, none of it would matter.

His hands gripped his hair, pulling just enough to cause pain and distract him from the ache in the back of his throat that just wanted him to use.

"Good morning." His mom knocked and entered. She wasn't overly cheerful like usual, instead she had puffy, red-rimmed eyes. "Are you sure you don't want me to go with you today?"

Davis squeezed his eyes shut. He was not ready to deal with his supportive and attentive mother, who had held his hand through rounds of chemotherapy and through intake into rehab. But right now, he wanted her to leave his room and maybe never talk to him again. If he had to see her, see the effort she had put into him, he would begin to feel guilty for his almost unquenchable desire to use.

"No." His voice was gravel and dust. "I need to do this alone."

"I'm going to go see Natalie and Cason this afternoon. Do you want to come?"

The question hurt his head even more. His chest burned and a flash of heat filled his belly. No, he didn't want to see Cason. He didn't want to think about her. Thinking about her only served as a reminder of the fact that he had ignored Alexis and her plea for help because of Cason.

Alexis might still be alive if . . . if.

God, he just wanted to get high.

But he did still want to see Cason.

"I'll see how I feel after the funeral."

"She's going to need friends. Has Mari been by to see her?"

Davis really needed his mother to stop asking him questions. To stop pushing. To stop.

"I think so," he managed. "I need to get dressed."

Amanda held his cheek. The warmth of her hand, more familiar than his own in some ways, filled him. Her touch had always been comfort. Warmth. Love. That's what his mom was. And he hated her for it. "Davis, you did everything you could for her."

He didn't say anything. He wanted to scream that he obviously hadn't, because she was dead.

"I'll call you after the funeral."

"Okay," Amanda conceded. She pressed a kiss to his forehead, and love and comfort rubbed his nerves like sandpaper on a sunburn.

chapter Twenty-Two

Cason was discharged from the hospital with a new set of forearm clip crutches (at least they were purple and not hospital silver) and three weeks off chemo to recover. She was fascinated by how light she felt now, in a physical sense. Her body was missing a major appendage and the heavy brace that had encased it. Her brain often thought of how it could do a *pirouette* much faster now. And then the fact that her leg was gone, therefore she was unable to spin, would overwhelm her soul.

"Cason, lunch." Natalie called to her, breaking her reverie. She came in with a plate full of food that Cason was sure would taste like sawdust.

"Thanks." She picked up a carrot stick and took a small bite to make her mom happy.

"Do you need a Percocet?" Her mom opened a bottle and had two pain pills ready for her.

"No, I'm good." She counted through the sharp pains that gripped her phantom toes, the strange sensations of an appendage that was gone. The pain meds made her sleepy, but never got rid of the weird feeling that her leg was still there when it most obviously wasn't.

"At least take some ibuprofen or something." Her mom tried again. "You need to stay ahead of the pain."

"I'm not in any pain," she lied, pushing away.

"You've barely eaten anything," her mother countered. "Remember what Dr. Henderson said about your weight."

"Well, I've lost a hell of a lot more than five pounds, Mom." Cason stood up, anger pulsing at the same tempo as the phantom pains, and motioned to where her leg was. "I'm going upstairs."

She wanted the world to be quiet.

Within moments of getting into bed, wrapping the worn feather comforter around her body and feeling the weight settle around her, there was a knock at her door.

"Cason? It's Mari."

Mari was quite literally the last person she wanted to see right now. But the one thing that Cason had learned in the few weeks that she had known Mari was that Mari was going to do exactly what she wanted. It didn't matter whether you wanted her to.

"Hey." Mari entered the room in one fluid motion, opening the door, moving in, closing the door, her crutches and disability never altering her stride. Cason hated that she noticed it. She hated that she knew that those simple movements weren't simple. She hated Mari. "I remember how bored I was after my amputation. I brought some things."

"Oh." Cason didn't want her there. She didn't want to see whatever things she'd brought. She wanted to bury her head and pretend that none of this happened.

She just wanted to dance.

Mari didn't seem to care that Cason didn't want her there. She sat on Cason's bed like they were lifelong friends, not people who had recently met at the cancer clinic. Mari opened her hot-pink, well-worn backpack. "My mom is the last person on earth who prints photos and puts albums together."

Cason didn't say anything, but she wanted to hurl all over the precious albums when she saw the pages filled with a very-bald Mari. Great, an entire photo album dedicated to Mari's cancer and amputation.

And in Cason's mind, now, those were the worst things in the absolute world.

"She made me bring these." Mari sighed. "She's currently downstairs with your mom, feeding her Papa's baklava and telling stories."

"Oh." Her mother had become a new person lately. Inviting cancer people over? It wouldn't surprise Cason if Natalie was calling Davis to hang out next.

"Yeah," Mari brushed if off like it was completely normal. "I wanted to show you these." She pulled out two large frames filled with collages of photos. Cason quickly realized they were from camp. "I guess Mama's not the only one to still print out pictures."

Cason didn't want to see any of these pictures. She didn't want to see that her life was going to go on. She knew it was. She knew that she couldn't get out of living this life with one leg. She just didn't have to do it smiling and acting like it was no big deal.

"This is me." Mari pointed to a photo of herself. "It's last summer."

"What are you doing?" Someone had taken this picture from the ground and Mari was clearly up in the air.

"It's the high ropes at camp." A faint smile crossed Mari's face. "I wanted to prove to Jase that I could do it without help."

"What are you doing exactly?" Cason could just make out the ropes and the harness holding her in.

"That particular element is like a rope bridge. I used the ropes at my sides to cross it." Mari's voice had grown soft with memory.

"That's . . . something." Cason thought it was unbelievably stupid to be that high up doing anything. Even if you had two legs.

"I didn't show you this so you could see just how awesome I am." Mari looked at Cason then. "I have never been a professional dancer. I didn't even take ballet classes as a kid because I wanted to play basketball like my brothers. I can never, ever, understand what you have lost, Cason." She paused then, checking her words. "But I do know what it's like to have one leg, to feel slightly put off and out of place in a world that's not at all built for you. I also know that it was while I was doing this, while I was strapped into a harness and belays with carabiners acting as the only thing that kept me from falling to my death, that I felt like I was dancing. Like I could float, in a way."

Cason didn't respond. She couldn't. Because her immediate thoughts were mean and unkind and not at all in the spirit of this visit from Mari. She wanted to yell and scream and say that Mari was right. She would never know exactly what Cason had lost.

Instead, she studied the pictures. There were a few funny pictures of Davis and Mari. "Is this Jase?" she asked, pointing to a picture of Mari and a tall boy.

"Yeah, that's from the gala that his mom puts on every year. I spoke at it last winter."

Cason was silent as she continued to look. Mari was with Jase in quite a few photos, from when they were much younger up to the one of them dancing at that formal event.

Cason had never really dated anyone. Dance didn't leave time for that. Whatever it was that had been going on with Davis, the one bright thing coming out of a terrible situation, seemed to have fizzled before it ever got fully lit. They hadn't talked in days. Maybe she was too scared to show him this side of her. Had it only been a week since he had kissed her? Why would he ever want to kiss her now? How would she ever date anyone now? What person would want to be with a disabled girl?

Stupid, ridiculous tears of self-pity flooded the back of her throat and forced their way up into her eyes. She shouldn't care about stupid crap like dating and boys and if she'd ever be found desirable.

"Until I dated Jase, I didn't think anyone would ever find me attractive." Mari said it so softly that Cason wasn't sure she was speaking at all. "I certainly never thought that Jason Ellison would love me." A small laugh. "You don't know our story, but he was, like, my long-time, completely unattainable crush." The laugh grew a little. "And somehow, here we are."

"Is it hard?" Cason managed to say the words around the tears. "Don't you hate it?"

Mari was quiet and thoughtful. She picked at the edges of the photo album and then drummed her fingers over some pictures in the collage. "There are parts of it that I do hate." Mari looked at Cason then. Her dark-brown eyes were wide, with honesty and truthfulness full in her face. "I won't lie about this. Being disabled, being an amputee and a cancer survivor? It's a really sucky thing sometimes.

"Friends will die. And you'll wonder why you didn't. It'll be different for you than it is for me. You'll be able to wear a prosthesis, and unless you want people to know that you had cancer, they'll never know. But you're always going to have a big reminder of it, Cason." Mari squeezed her eyes shut tight and shook her head, the brown curls falling around her face. "I used to get so mad at Jase and Davis. They never had to tell anyone that they'd had cancer and *everyone* knew I had. It became part of my identity without my permission.

"And people will treat you differently. Like you're fragile, or that you accomplished something so great that it should be a book." Mari opened her eyes. "What people don't understand is that we are literally just doing what we have to do. We aren't special. We aren't some chosen breed of cancer fighters. We're no better than anyone else."

"We just got a really shitty Uno hand," Cason whispered to herself as much as to Mari. "Is it hard dating Jase?"

"You mean Mr. Perfect?" Mari arched a perfectly shaped brow. "No, because he loves me for all of my stupidity and cockiness. The things that are hard with dating have nothing to do with my disability."

Cason didn't believe that at all.

"I know, I'd think I was a liar too," Mari laughed. "For him, my disability was never a problem. For others, it was, but that's another story."

"But, how do you do things?"

"Like sex?"

Cason flushed immediately. "Not sex, well, not really . . . but, how could anyone ever find me attractive like this?"

Mari was quiet, and Cason realized that what she'd said was probably insulting, but she didn't have the energy to care. "I've often wondered the same thing." Mari's smile was all sarcasm and no mirth. "And I'm not saying Jase solved all my problems and all my fears about having one leg. He had to practically beat me over the head until I started to believe that it really didn't matter."

"But he gets all of the cancer stuff." Frustration filled Cason's chest, like the way soda fizzed up after being shaken. "He doesn't care about that."

"You haven't actually met Jase or his family or know much about him outside these photos. But he doesn't care, not because he's a cancer kid, but because he's a decent human." Mari's ire was building. "A decent human will want to be with you because of who you are, not because of or despite your disability. I promise, you'll see." Mari seemed to be studying Cason, looking past the anger and inconsiderate words.

"When you're ready, I'll help you learn to navigate this world. I have lived with my disability a little longer than you."

Cason just nodded. She didn't have any words or thoughts to add. She hated that she would need tips from Mari. She hated the way that Mari said disability like it was a hair color, not the terrible, life-changing thing it was.

She hated everything.

"Have you seen much of Davis?" Mari changed the subject, maybe suspecting Cason's irritations. "I know he was going to the funeral today."

"Wait, what?" For the first time in days, Cason was pulled from her self-pity circle. "What funeral?"

"Alexis, his ex, OD'd the other day." Mari said it like it was common knowledge. "He didn't tell you?"

"No." And maybe that said everything about their relationship.

chapter Twenty-Three

Davis could see the silver coffin at the front of the church from where he stood behind the last pew. He'd been to funerals before. Hell, he'd been to friends' funerals before. Cancer meant you lost people you were close to. That was just a fact.

But knowing Alexis was lying in that casket was too much.

Because it was his fault.

The closer he got to the front, where she was, where her parents greeted the other mourners, the more he fought his own soul.

"Davis." Alexis's mother took him in her arms and hugged him fiercely. "You tried so hard. We all did." His words stayed clenched together in his heart, jabbed there with the hypodermic needles he'd helped Alexis shoot up with. He hugged her back. He was a fraud and should play the part. When they parted, Mrs. Foster dripped tears onto his suit coat. "Go say goodbye."

Alexis didn't look right. Her hair and makeup were soft. A light touch had been given, but enough that you couldn't see the damage the drugs had done. In all the funerals he'd been to, cancer had wrecked the person. But Alexis truly looked like she could just be asleep. He looked at the items in the casket. A photo from when Alexis had been a cheerleader. Letters to her from friends. And Davis mentally begged her chest to move.

Just breathe.

Just do it.

Just breathe once.

Do it.

But there was nothing but the shell of the girl that he had killed.

He retreated to his seat, straining in the church pew to find something to ease his discomfort. Instead, he was unwelcome in his own body.

God, he wanted to use.

"Alexis was only starting in life," the preacher spoke and Davis choked on bile. He wasn't sure when the service had even started. Why was he even there? He tried to focus on the words that were being said, the verses about the poor inheriting the earth, the blessing of the unfortunate. There was a lot of praise for her parents who had tried to fix her.

Fix her.

He should have called her back. He should have written her. He should have done *something* to show she wasn't alone in her recovery. Instead, he'd been too wrapped up in fighting his own cravings and fixing the other people around him.

Hurting everyone in his path.

Unwelcome and unhurried tears slid down his face. He wiped at them, scratching his face in the process, happy to feel something other than the gaping sadness that filled him.

"The Fosters are the type of parents children dream of." Davis wanted to throw up apologies all over her parents, to show how much he hated that he'd led her down this path. He might not have handed her the heroin that eventually killed her, but he might as well have.

They hadn't been able to save Alexis. They had tried. He wanted to scream and yell and tell everyone that only Alexis could save herself.

He couldn't fix her.

But he could get his fix.

~

He didn't stay for the burial. Instead, he began walking right as the sky opened with rain.

"Davis." That voice knotted Davis's stomach in flashes of heat and a deep tug in his gut.

"It's a shame about Alexis." Footsteps splashing against wet pavement caught up from behind him. This couldn't be a coincidence.

"Yeah." Davis shoved his hands in his pockets. Or he might beg Ethan for just one pill. Then he'd take that pill and crush it as fine as he could, maybe he'd find an old pipe. More than likely, he'd snort it. God, he could feel the burn and the acrid taste flow down his throat. Davis could have said something about the temporary protection order, or the fact that the police had been looking for Ethan, but he didn't.

Because if Davis did, Ethan might leave.

And if Ethan left, he would take the dope with him.

"It's too bad about Alexis." Ethan said again. He smiled mournfully with his perfectly straight teeth, and he looked like any other twenty-something white guy.

Ethan may have been the weapon, but Davis had been the killer. *You killed her.* New words echoed through his head. No longer was it just the repetitive theme of wanting to use, it was a hard voice that didn't whisper, but snarled his darkest fears. *Maybe you should die too.* He quickened his pace toward home, just two more blocks away. Two unfathomably, impossibly far blocks away.

"It's burning through you right now, I can tell." Ethan slung his arm around Davis like they were old friends, bringing them to a halt in the drizzle. "There's no need to suffer in pain. Why don't you let me help you? We can forget all about that warrant for my arrest and just party in remembrance of our girl."

Davis immediately felt shameful and dirty. He moved away, but not too quickly. He wasn't sure if his next steps were to run or follow.

Why hadn't the police picked up Ethan yet?

Maybe Detective Avery didn't really care about his case.

Maybe it was low on his priority list because Davis had a rap sheet.

Maybe Davis should just go with Ethan.

A car pulled up beside them. Did Ethan plan this? To kidnap him, drug him, shoot him? All the options sounded horrifying and tempting at the same time. The window rolled down. "Davis?"

"John." Davis's voice cracked over the name of his sponsor. The sponsor whom he'd only ever called by his last name.

"Need a lift?" Mr. Williams may have sprouted wings just then. It was too good of an offer to deny.

"Yes."

"Next time, Davis." Ethan waved, ending in a finger point that resembled a gun.

Davis knew there would be a next time.

He knew because he'd just made it too easy for Ethan. That one pause in eye contact, that one indistinct signal that said *maybe* was enough for a drug dealer to pounce.

chapter Twenty-Four

Rain poured, streaking the window in weird crisscrossing shapes. Cason breathed out, watching as her breath formed a perfect circle on the window. Stupid tears slid down her cheeks. Again. All she did was cry. She wanted to blame it on the pain meds, but she couldn't. To blame them, you'd have to take them, and she refused.

"Cason, you have a guest." Natalie knocked and poked her head in. Davis was right behind her.

"Hi." He was in a dark-gray, rain-spattered suit. His hair was wet, but not soaked.

"Hey," she replied in a deadpan tone that covered her smiles, her heart, and the somersaults her stomach once did. Davis still stood in the doorway of her room. Natalie left, giving them some space to talk. "Come in."

"Thanks."

If she'd been less self-absorbed, she might have seen that Davis was upset. That his eyes were red and puffy. That he was on the verge of collapse. That she should feel bad for avoiding him when he'd lost someone.

But cancer and an amputation that ruined your life meant she was done with sympathy. It meant she only noticed the fact that he was interrupting her self-imposed isolation. She only felt irritation at the fact that he seemed to need something from her that she didn't have in her to give.

Davis sat in the desk chair near her bed. It was the first time he'd been in her room. He took in the décor. She knew what he saw: the busted pointe shoes hanging like a chandelier in one corner, the pictures of her in various dances, from her early days in toddler movement class to her last performance as the sugar plum fairy in *The Nutcracker*.

"Are you okay?" His voice was strangely quiet. Not the Davis that had beaten her soundly at Uno. Not the Davis that had held her head as she puked. Not the one that had held her gently as they danced. Some other incarnation that she didn't know.

"Sure." *No!* her brain screamed. *Can't you see I'm broken?*

He moved to her then, sitting on the bed, the stiffness of his suit wrinkling next to her small frame. She was emaciated from not eating and the chemo and she knew she should care. She knew that she should want to get better and to be more, but she didn't care.

His arm went around her and he pulled her close. Her head fell onto his chest with the thump of his heart under her ear. His hand felt cool on the back of her head and neck. He held her.

And once again, she cried.

And if she'd paid any attention, she would have felt his tears too.

chapter Twenty-Five

Tears moved down his nose, over his chin, and slid onto Cason's head. She was dripping her own tears into his dress shirt. He hadn't bothered to change.

The hiss in his brain slid over his cervical spine and down to his toes. The need that had almost overtaken him after the funeral filled his lungs again. There was a desperate want, a hunger that ached in his bones.

Get high.

Just once.

It will all feel so much better.

"Are you okay?" Cason pulled back. "I got your coat wet."

"What?" His brain buzzed, returning from his ulterior thoughts.

"Mari stopped by." Her words were stilted, and she worked each word around her tongue. "She told me about the funeral."

He didn't want to get into it. He didn't want to tell her that Alexis was gone. That her demons, her disease, had just been too damn much.

That he'd failed her.

That he failed everyone.

"I'm sorry." She said it because it was what you were supposed to say. He wasn't even sure she understood. "Is there anything I can do?"

"No." And he didn't elaborate. Because if he did, he would tell her about Ethan and he would tell her how easy it would be to score, to use again. And dear God, it would feel so much better if he could just get high. Just forget. Just pulse with the high of dope.

God, he hated his own brain.

He wanted to claw at his mind, rake his nails down the synapses and neurons as they fired, and he begged to just forget everything in his own head.

And now he was in Cason's room.

Holding her.

Weeping with her.

And still the only thing he could think was;

Just once.

He eyed a bottle of pills on her nightstand.

Clenching his fist, Davis bit the inside of his cheek, needing to feel a physical pain to match the one coursing through his veins.

He looked at the bottle once more.

He closed his eyes.

And prayed the Serenity Prayer once more.

God grant me the serenity to accept the things I cannot change,

   courage to change the things I can,

and the wisdom to know the difference.
Davis was sober.
Still.

chapter Twenty-Six

Phantom pains were a bitch. That's all Cason could think, the next day. Her time had been consumed with getting through one phantom pain only to be hit by another. She could feel her non-existent knee pulling now. She tried breathing through them like some sort of Lamaze exercise, but it made her feel stupid. Holding onto the end of her residual limb, she massaged gently. The tissue was still very tender from the amputation. She clenched her teeth, trying her best to make the pain stop.

Giving up, she moved, walking anywhere in an attempt to get away from the frustrating and painful sensations. She crutched down the stairs, slowly, and saw her mom sitting on the floor. Her phone was pressed to her chest and silent sobs wrenched through her.

"Mom?" Cason moved as quickly as she could. Alarm and panic raced through her.

"Oh!" Her mom pulled Cason into a bear hug that nearly knocked the breath from her. "Cason."

"What is it?" she demanded again.

"The pathology from your tumor."

"What?" It was like her mom was speaking Latin suddenly.

"Your tumor. It was dead."

"What?"

"There was no active disease. The chemo had destroyed it."

"I don't understand." Cason moved away and sat next to her mom on the ground. She tried to make sense of all the words her mother had been saying, but it was like gibberish.

"The tests on your tumor came back, and there were no cancer cells that were alive."

"And this is good news, right?"

"Yes," her mom laughed through tears. "This is great news."

"So why are you crying?"

"Dr. Lee talked me through what happened in your surgery a bit more."

"Oh." Cason's reprieve of happiness passed like a cloud over the sun. Her bones grew cold at the mention of Dr. Lee's name. The phantom pains resurged.

"Cason, they wouldn't have been able to do a successful salvage."

"What?" Again, Latin.

"You would have needed a complete hip, femur, and knee replacement. You wouldn't have been able to dance."

She let those words sit in her head. No running. No

jumping. No ballet, for sure. "So, I was never really going to be at the *barre* again, either way."

"Not in the way we'd wanted."

"It was always going to end like this, even if I hadn't fallen." She motioned to the open space where her once-limitless leg was.

"Yes."

"Fuck." Cason bit the word off. Then she cried.

Again.

~

Her nerves did a *bourrée,* little steps so fast that they looked like a whirl, across her stomach lining that filled Cason with dread. She hated everything about what she was about to do. She didn't want to go to physical therapy. She didn't want to prepare her body to use a prosthesis and to rebuild the muscle that she had lost over the past months of disease and chemotherapy.

Kelsey, with her long, dark hair and perfectly toned body, made Cason want to throw things. Kelsey was going to be Cason's *fantastic* and *wonderful* physical therapist, Mari had promised. Cason hated her at first sight. Kelsey stood in the lobby, smiling too happily at Natalie and then turning all watts of the smile in Cason's direction.

"I cannot wait to get you up and going on your new leg!" Kelsey was all cheer and excitement. "We're going to do awesome things! In no time, we're going to have you performing again."

Fuck that.

If there was one thing Cason was certain of, it was that her last performance had been in the audition room in front of the professionals from ABT.

Nothing this perky, manic pixie dream girl said would convince Cason otherwise.

Cason thought about crying again. She thought about crying a lot these days.

She had cried on Davis.

She had cried on Mari.

And in this moment, she thought about crying again.

But it had nothing to do with pain or even the emotional pull of no longer having a leg.

Instead, she stood in front of a full-length mirror.

She stood in front of the mirror and held onto a *barre.*

"Just balance," Kelsey said. Cason had a balance belt wrapped around her waist twice. Kelsey held onto it tightly just in case she nose-dived.

Cason tried not to look at her body. She didn't want to study her frame in the mirror like she had once done, checking for posture, fingers, feet and hip positions.

She most definitely did not want to see where her left leg just ended. That rounded stump of a leg. No matter that everyone called it a residual limb, she knew that it was a stump. Something that used to be more . . . so much more.

"How does it feel?" Kelsey picked up the hand that

Cason had been gripping the *barre* with. "Think you can let go?"

"Yeah." This was stupid. She could balance indefinitely. She used to stand on her big toe in an *arabesque* for fun.

"Don't turn your hips out." Kelsey squared her body for her, running her hands down Cason's hips, over her stump. She briefly thought of slapping the therapist, but knew that wasn't a smart choice. "What kind of ab workout are you doing?"

"What?" Cason practically laughed.

"Your prosthesis is going to pull on all parts of your body, not just your residual limb. Plus, you're a dancer and I want you to start thinking like one again. That means strength training and working out."

"I still have at least six months of chemo left." Cason started to argue.

"And nowhere in your protocol does it say you should become a couch cushion. Netflix is cool and all, but we want you back at the *barre*."

Cason's jaw dropped. Who in the hell did this woman think she was? Heat moved over her face, her stomach, filling her chest. She wasn't sure if it was rage or self-pity. "I'm not going to be some inspiring story for the hospital." The words were spit with venom and contempt. "I danced with the Atlanta Ballet Conservatory. I was accepted into the American Ballet Theatre's Studio program."

"I'm aware of these things, Cason." Kelsey picked up

her crutches and handed them to her. "And while ABT might be too stuffy to realize you are a better and more interesting dancer now, you are still a dancer and I expect you to act like it."

"You are not my director," she hissed over the pain and frustration that was building in her heart. Each thrum of her heart pushed and pulsed with anger and sadness.

"No," Kelsey said as she lifted a perfectly arched brow. "I'm worse. Because what I want you to accomplish is more than just a beautiful *attitude* or *jeté*. I know what it takes to be a dancer, and I expect that same type of determination in your PT with me."

Cason didn't say anything in response. She didn't want to talk about dance. She didn't want to see what her body looked like now. She didn't want to do anything that even remotely felt like dance.

Because when she danced, she flew.

And all she felt now was the lead in her soul, the heaviness that weighed down her body in ways she couldn't quite describe. It was like when they'd amputated her leg, they'd also taken her wings.

chapter Twenty-Seven

Davis had promised Cason he'd stop by her physical therapy session, but it seemed like lately, he was letting her down in every way that mattered. He didn't share what he was thinking with her because her life was just as painful as his. How could he compare the constant need to use or the guilt that he felt about Alexis with Cason's loss? When he walked into the room, Cason was so focused on moving up the stairs that she didn't hear him. It still shocked him to see her with one leg. She looked small and frail now. Even before, when she'd had the brace on, she'd still seemed so formidable. Now she was tired. Her body was curved, her normally straight spine with perfect posture was hunched over her crutches and the stairs. It was almost like she was hugging herself as she moved, trying to find comfort in this new body.

"Hey." He walked over to where she balanced on the set of stairs, her new crutches hanging from her arms as she contemplated the next step.

A watery smile played on her lips. "I'm not happy today."

"You don't have to be." He sat down on the top step, pulling her down with him.

"I feel . . ." He watched as she searched for words. "Different."

"Cason, you're still you." He tried to find the words that would ease her heart. But it was so hard to hear anything over his own need.

His own shame.

His own guilt.

"No." She wiped at a stray tear and runny nose. "I'm not, Davis." She looked at him, her sad eyes filling her wan face. "I'm not a whole person anymore. I'm only part of one."

"You don't really think that."

"I do." She chewed at her lip until it was red and nearly bleeding. "I thought I'd dance again." Agitation coated her words. "I really did."

"You still can." He pressed his head to hers, filling her space, making sure she heard him.

"Are you listening to me?" Her face was splotched with red. "I was a perfect dancer. I had feet that my own mother envied. Dancing was my *life*. Every goal, every ambition I've ever had was about dance. It was my only future, and every day I'm reminded how it was ripped away from me." Her shoulders curled in. "It's all I've known, all I ever was."

"You still can be."

"I will never tie on pointe shoes or dance the Lincoln Center." She moaned the words and doubled over. "I am broken and I hate this." She looked back up at him. "I hate you." She drilled holes into him. "I am not some broken doll you can fucking fix."

"I don't think anything is wrong with you." Her vicious words settled into his mind. "I think you're hurt." It was all his fault.

Somehow it was all his fault.

"I can't do this right now." She stood, moving slowly down the stairs, away from him, and toward the waiting room. "I can't be with you."

Hearing her words, he got up and ran to her, stopping her gently. "What do you mean?"

"I can't be your girlfriend or whatever." She pushed his hands off her arms. "You deserve someone . . ." More tears; he was so tired of seeing her cry, of making her cry. "Someone who is whole."

Her words sliced through him more efficiently than any surgeon's scalpel or drug dealer's knife. They hit every artery and organ as they tore through his bruised flesh. He didn't move after Cason as she crutched from the room. He couldn't. How could he when he was bleeding all over the floor?

Just one hit.

chapter Twenty-Eight

"Cason?" Her mother called up the stairs. "We've got therapy."

She was the one who had therapy, not her mother. Natalie was forcing Cason to meet with a shrink. Cason didn't want to talk about any of this. She wanted to hide in her room and sleep. When she was asleep, she was still able to dance. Her turnout was perfect, her feet never ached, and her muscles were never sore. She soared when she made her leaps, she floated over the floor as she moved across it in a *pas de chat,* and when she woke . . . there was nothing.

Literally.

No, that wasn't quite right. There was something. There was the constant reminder that her leg was gone. The endless tingling in her foot that was no longer there, alive and well in her mind like a cruel joke. She found the only way to soothe the constant tingles, the weird shooting sensations that went through the arch of her nonexistent foot, the throbbing pain of her ankle, was to move her present foot. She wriggled it, twisted it, pretended she was *en pointe* going from first position to *relevé.*

The sensations were too much for her to handle on her own, and nothing she took would touch them.

~

Her shrink's office was different than what she'd expected. The office was supposed to be calming, with a waterfall and a zen garden that Cason thought about etching curse words in to. None of it did anything for her.

"Hi, Cason. I'm Dr. Keller."

Cason looked up from the couch she was sitting on. She wondered whether she was supposed to lie down. She didn't say anything back, she just nodded to let the lady know she'd heard her.

"Want anything to drink? I've got sodas and water."

"No." She marked the choreography of *Romeo and Juliet* in her mind so she didn't have to pay attention. Cason was an unwilling participant in this therapy session.

"You don't want to be here, huh?"

She studied the doctor, really looking at her for the first time. She was young, tall, probably had been an athlete at some point. Dark–brown, massive curls hung down her back, and she had brown skin and deep, brown eyes. "No, but . . ." There was too much rolling through her brain to ever begin to explain.

"Why don't you tell me why you think your mom set this up?"

"Probably because Dr. H said to."

Dr. Keller smiled. "Why did Dr. H suggest this, then?"

"Because I'm depressed."

"Are you?"

"What do you think?" Cason laughed sarcastically. "About four months ago, I was dancing the audition of my life. Now I'm missing a leg. A *grand jeté* is not in my future."

"That's not fair."

"It's not, is it?" She ran a hand over her residual limb, trying to ease the ache of the phantom pains. "It hurts."

"Physically?"

"Yes." Cason was still trying to rub out the pain. "And no."

"It's more than your body."

"It's everything."

"Well, let's talk about everything."

chapter Twenty-nine

Just one hit. The burning smell of glass and ground pills filled his nose. His hand could feel the glass as it heated and hear the slight gurgle as the smoke filled his mouth, nose, brain. *All you need is one.*

"Davis?" His mom came into the room with a half-empty laundry basket. A cover to come in.

"I'm getting up." His voice hurt, rough against his throat, like he'd swallowed crushed concrete.

"Work today?" She put away his clothes and tried not to look concerned. The line between her eyes had always been her tell, his way of knowing exactly how worried she was. Lately, it had been there constantly.

It had been a month since he'd kissed Cason.

Three weeks since her surgery.

Two weeks since Alexis's funeral.

"Hospital and then the café." He stretched and thought about helping, but didn't. His brain was still screaming. *One hit. One hit! ONE HIT!*

"You've been busy lately."

"Trying to stay out of trouble." School had officially been out a week. And his previous plans of spending the whole time with Cason had been obliterated when she'd stormed out of his life.

"How's that working out for you?" She turned then, concern, compassion, love, and just a little distrust on her face. Eyes that were his, ones he knew that saw straight through his lies.

"Just let up, Mom," he snapped, and wanted to regret it but didn't.

"Davis . . ." She started toward him.

"Stop suffocating me!" The words were hard and rough like the gravel that lived in his stomach. "I need to get dressed." He narrowed his eyes. "I do have work. You can call Ike if you want."

"I will." She leveled him with a look.

"God, I thought you trusted me." He pushed the covers up, dragging his sleepy body from the bed. His brain screamed at him for every move.

"I do." She took his face in her hands. "It's your disease I don't trust."

He didn't look at her. He didn't want her to read his face, his anger and distrust of his own mind. "I'll get through it."

"I know you will." His mom started to leave his room, but stopped in the doorway. "Maybe you should see John today." It wasn't a request.

Just one hit.

~

"Davis." Mr. Williams walked into the Daily Grind. "Take a break?"

It was the last thing Davis wanted to do.

He wanted to run and score.

"Mr. Williams," Davis said, sitting down across from his school counselor. He drummed his fingers on the table in front of him, feeling the fake wood under each finger. He did his best to let each finger hit one at a time, but at a face pace, quick and frenetic, the way his brain felt.

"Are we back to that?" The older man smiled. "I thought after the other day we'd moved on."

A piece of a smile quirked the side of his mouth, but never made it all the way there. He didn't have the emotions or the energy to feel anything right now that wasn't somehow tainted with sorrow and sadness. "A momentary lapse."

"How are you doing?"

All the words that he wanted to use to describe his current situation were negative, not a moment of happiness or joy in his brain. His need to use burned with an intensity that he hadn't experienced since his days in rehab. And God, that had sucked so damn much. This wasn't much better.

"Okay," he lied.

"Has there been any movement in your case?"

"Not that I've heard." Davis didn't even know where the bitterness that laced his words came from. He hadn't realized that he was mad that Ethan was still out walking the streets. Maybe if the police would do their damn jobs and arrest him then Davis wouldn't feel this undeniable and painful urge to find him. Maybe the constant pull to use would be tempered if Ethan was unreachable.

"Patience is hard. I don't understand how something like this works, but I'm sure the police are doing their job," Mr. Williams said. "How long have you been sober, Davis?"

Davis's brain fizzled at the question. *Long enough* was his first thought. How long had he been sober? Right now, his thoughts were crowded, filled with anger and resentment, and if he let himself think too long, probably fear.

John took out a mangled piece of paper. Davis knew what was inside, knew already what was scrawled in barely legible words.

It was Davis's wish list. Or prayer list, or whatever.

"I want you to look this over, think about it, and then let's meet again."

Davis didn't say much. He didn't touch the paper that now sat in front of him. It was worn, the edges of the paper cottony with use and being stuck in a pocket.

"Take your time. Look at your list. And remember why you've fought so hard these last nine months."

"Nine months and fifteen days." Eyes closed and head tucked in, Davis tried to think of a way to make all the aches go away. He couldn't make Cason better. He couldn't make Alexis better. He couldn't even make himself better right now.

Could he?

chapter Thirty

Physical therapy once again had been complete and utter bullshit.

But at least this time, she hadn't broken up with her boyfriend while at it.

Kelsey, the woman who was supposedly going to help Cason walk again, was possibly the Antichrist. Or maybe just a bitch. Either way, Cason did not want to work with her again. She didn't want to see her ridiculous perky face or the way that her hands held onto the *barre* effortlessly.

It wasn't lost on Cason that Kelsey was a dancer. She might be a physical therapist now, but at some point, she'd danced. Her posture, her feet, they told the story. And Cason hated her for it. Because Kelsey could go back to dancing anytime she wanted. She could walk into any class and dance.

Cason couldn't walk at all.

She would never dance like she had.

She didn't care how many inspirational videos people sent her. Cason would never be able to dance like she had.

"How did it go?" Mari was in her room. Friends dropping by to see her was a new thing that happened now.

The irony that she'd lost a leg but gained friends was not lost on Cason. "Kelsey is super fun at camp."

"I think I must have seen someone else." Cason flopped back on her bed, pillows engulfing her body. "That woman is a bitch."

"She can be pushy."

"I'm used to pushy. This woman borders on cruel."

"Have you talked to Davis?" Mari had made it clear that even though they'd broken up, Cason was still her friend. That she wasn't choosing sides or anything like that.

"No." Cason pulled the pillow over her head, not wanting to see her friend. "I wasn't very nice."

"You're both dealing with a lot of shit." Cason felt Mari lie back on the pillows with her. "But, if you think about it, maybe shoot him a text."

"Don't you think that'd be weird?" Cason lifted the edge of one pillow, peaking out at her friend. "I mean, I have zero relationship experience, but texting your ex? Because he's having a crappy day?"

"Part of it is selfish." Mari laughed a little. "I don't want things to be awkward at camp, and if you two can't talk, it'll be awkward, and then I'll be forced to choose sides, and I'll choose you because you're in my cabin and you're my friend. And even though Davis was my friend first, you're going to live with me and could shave my head in my sleep or something."

Cason was quiet for a second before a peal of laughter

filled her, welled up, and broke through like she couldn't have stopped it if she'd wanted to.

It startled her a little because it was her first real, spontaneous laugh in quite a while. And yet, there it was, filling the air around her and clinging to her weary soul. Hallelujah, laughing was good medicine, and she now hated every inspirational poster in the history of ever. And that just made her laugh harder.

Hiding in the depths of her heart, somewhere that was the size of a tiny firefly, Cason felt a little hope.

~

Cason stood in her closet, crutches clamped around her arms, and pulled at clothes she hadn't worn since before her diagnosis. She'd lost so much weight that her old clothes hung on her frame, and now that the brace around her leg was gone, there was nothing to help hold up her yoga pants. She flipped dresses out, muttering about them fitting wrong. Taking some old jeans out of the closet, she stuffed them in a donation bag. She had plans to sit down at her computer that night with her mother's credit card to order whatever she wanted. If cancer didn't give you that pass, she didn't know what did.

And that's when she saw them.

Something that had been totally innocuous her entire life.

Two shoes, sitting side by side on the floor of her closet. Not even a pair of damn toe shoes. Just plain old ballet flats. Leopard print with a teal insole, a black ribbon around the edge, and a tiny little string bow on the toe. They weren't even her favorite shoes. They were just some stupid shoes that had been sitting on the floor of her closet, collecting dust.

And waiting to mock her in this moment.

Cason slowly sat down on the floor of her closet and picked up the shoes, examining both of them as if they held some sort of weird secret. She ran her finger around the toe of the left shoe, wondering if she could feel the imprint her toes had once made. She'd probably never worn the shoes enough to even make that happen.

She threw the shoes across the room, wishing they would break into a million little pieces and that it would magically make her feel better like it did in the movies.

chapter Thirty-one

"Hi, Detective Avery, it's Davis Channing." His palm was sweating as he held the phone against his ear. He paused, clearing his throat, and then tried to speak with some authority. "I was calling to see what the status of my case was. I know we talked the other week after I ran into Ethan outside Alexis Foster's funeral. Please call me back with an update." He left the voicemail and hoped that he didn't sound too needy. Davis didn't want the detective to know just how shaky his grasp on his sobriety was.

Right now, he felt like he was on a tightrope, and the tiniest of breezes was going to knock him off, send him spinning and spiraling into a hole he might not climb out of.

They don't care. Davis's addiction whispered false words about the police, his parents, anyone who might be of help to him.

They never have.

You know how to make this go away.

Make it all go away.

Davis turned up the volume in his car, hoping to drown out his own brain. He had to go to the hospital. It was his day to work, and he couldn't leave them in a lurch. Heather would never forgive him and she would probably tell Mari, who would have no problem telling his parents if she thought he was in trouble.

He could still see Mari's tear-streaked face, the way she had looked at him last year, so hurt and angry.

"You're throwing your life away." She hadn't yelled, which he probably would have preferred. She was soft and just sounded sad. "I can't watch another friend die, Davis."

"Don't," he'd snarled. "I can't believe you told my parents that I'm a dopehead."

"You mean you're not?" She crutched closer and sniffed the sleeve of his shirt. "You smell like crap."

Davis had wanted to slug her.

And that's when he knew that he did have a problem.

He had nearly hit a person. Someone he was close to. Someone who was only trying to help him.

"I don't need your help, Mari." But even as he'd said the words, he'd known it was a lie. "Go screw Jase and leave me alone."

"I'm going to let that slide." Her dark-brown eyes had narrowed. "We all know that there's something going on. We all know that you have a problem. I'm just the only one with the balls to say something. So here's the deal, Davis, get clean before camp in two weeks, and I'll forget this conversation ever happened. You show up to camp high or looking like you might be trying to score, and I will not hesitate to tell Dr. H."

"Fuck off." He'd rarely felt the kind of terror that was

spiraling in his stomach like he did right then. Mari telling Dr. H was the next level. He'd pushed past his closest friend right then, wanting to push her down with every ounce of his being, but somehow, he had showed the tiniest bit of restraint. He'd left Mari standing outside his house, the house she had just left because she was telling his parents she thought he had a drug problem.

He didn't really remember the conversation he'd had with his parents that evening. He was sure it was full of lies. Of him telling them that Mari was just a drama queen. That she was jealous of him for some reason. That he was fine, that he'd just been sick lately, reminding them that his grades had been fine and that he'd had a job.

But he did remember his parents' faces two weeks later when they'd bailed him out of jail after being caught with pills that "didn't belong" to him and arrested for possession with intent to distribute. He remembered all of that with a sickening clarity.

Maybe if he could forget it then he would have already gotten high, and instead of feeling like shit about his life, he would have the slightly fuzzy feeling, the warm and comforting feeling of being so high that he could float. If he could forget the way the cuffs had felt on his wrists, the way the cops had pushed and pulled, not caring if he'd been injured, then maybe he'd have scored already. If he could just forget the look on his mom's face when she'd held his hand as they checked him into a detox center, the pain and sickness that had followed those days.

Maybe if he could forget some of that, he wouldn't have to deal with the intense feelings of guilt and sadness that seemed to be filling him.

He parked in the hospital lot and sat in his car. Deep breaths. He begged his body to pull it together. He needed to get his act together, to not feel so much right now.

Sitting on the passenger seat, like it was the most important passenger in his car, was the list that John had given him.

He closed his eyes, and before he could stop himself, he opened the fragile paper, opened his eyes, and stared at his own handwriting.

Reasons to Stay Sober

1. Because I'll die if I don't.

2. Because I want to.

3. Mom/Dad

4. Dr. H

5. Camp

I need a hit . . .

~

He slowly walked down the stairs of the parking garage to the ground floor, and stopped when he saw a woman sitting on the stairs. Mrs. Martin wiped her eyes, trying desperately to hold it together.

"Mrs. Martin?" He walked to help her up. "Are you hurt?"

"No." She tried to stifle the sob. "I was just headed back to the clinic." She looked at Davis quietly, really seeing him. She blushed, wiped a tear, and hiccupped a little over her words. "You've been nice to her, Davis." He didn't say anything, but stood there, his hands in his pockets. "You listen to her. I don't."

"You just want what is best for her." It wasn't at all what he actually thought most of the time.

"I'm bad at listening to her." She rubbed her eyes, and her black mascara smeared. "I didn't listen before she had cancer. Maybe if I had . . ." She drew a shaky breath and looked at him. Natalie Martin crumbled again. Fresh tears filled her eyes, and her breath staggered over her words. "I wanted her to dance."

"Cason will find ways to dance, Mrs. Martin." He didn't know what to do. "Or she'll find something else."

Natalie silently pulled a crumpled, stale tissue from her purse, sending dust flying everywhere. She looked at the tissue and then out the cinder-block window that overlooked the parking lot. "I know that something happened between you two."

He shoved his hands in his pockets and felt the regret coating the lining of his chest. "Yeah, she's in a tough space right now."

Natalie Martin was seeing someone other than a junkie for the first time. The irritation that had lived in her eyes when he was present was now gone. Instead, she looked at him with an openness, and maybe a little regret. "She is," Natalie sniffed. "She lost more than her leg. She lost her future."

"But she'll find a new one. Cason is too driven to let something sidetrack her." And it was true. Cason had accomplished more in her life than he ever could.

"You're a good friend for her." Natalie spoke haltingly, like she hated admitting the words out loud. "And I'm bad at being a parent sometimes." She met his eyes. "And I'm sorry I was so horrid when we first met."

"You only saw a junkie." He couldn't meet her eyes anymore, because he still was a junkie.

"You and your friends have been kind to her." Natalie stood then. "I'm still not sure that camp is something I want her to go to. But, if you have any other friends, maybe an amputee who wears a prosthesis, it might help Cason somehow."

"I'll give Noah a call." A wry smile pulled at his face; it felt unfamiliar, like he was out of practice with the gesture. "He's an athlete too."

"That would be nice." And together, they walked down the steps. The ache to use released the grip that it had on his body for days now. It eased just enough that he felt like he could finally breathe, could finally feel the sun, feel the summer heat on his body.

For the first time in a while, a tiny spark of hope lit in his belly.

chapter Thirty-Two

It was July, and Cason was bundled into the thickest sweatshirt she could find, but not even that helped the chills as they shook her feverish body. The hospital blanket wasn't doing much. She sat shaking in the lobby, waiting for them to be ready to take her blood and see exactly where her counts were. If her white count was too low, she knew she'd end up in the hospital.

And though she would deny it until the end of her days, with the way she felt right now, maybe the hospital wouldn't be so bad. She pulled the blanket up under her chin, trying any way she could to fight the chills. Her head ached, her phantom pains were worse than they usually were, and she just wanted to go to sleep. Her mom was nowhere in sight.

And then she was walking in with Davis.

They weren't talking, but Davis had a hand on her mom's elbow, helping her into the lobby area. Cason watched, bewildered, as Natalie smiled—yes, a little stiffly—at Davis before sitting down. "How are you feeling?"

Cason looked at Davis. Their eyes locked and she

wanted to bury herself in his warmth. He was always so warm.

"Crappy," she said instead, her teeth chattering. She wanted to ask more questions to find out why Natalie was with Davis, why she'd been nearly pleasant to him. But the thoughts only hurt her head, made her brain ache and twirl with lack of direction. The questions moved to the back of her brain, walking away at the same pace Davis did. He didn't give her a wave goodbye or come closer to talk to her, instead he smiled sadly and left the lobby of the clinic.

Sitting in the chair, still waiting to be called back to the triage area, she let her head fall onto her mother's shoulder.

Something she couldn't remember doing.

Ever.

~

"Well, Ms. Martin, you have your first fever." Dr. H slid his stethoscope out of his ears and gave her a friendly smile. "You feel pretty bad, huh?"

"Yeah." She still shivered. The meds they'd given her hadn't quite kicked in yet.

"I don't see any signs of immediate infection." Dr. H felt along the lymph nodes in her throat before moving to tap his fingers on her sinuses. His hands were cold, but also somehow weirdly comforting, like she knew she was being taken care of by the best. "Your white count is extremely low."

"Gross." Cason groaned. "Is that why I feel so bad?"

"Yeah, a weakened immune system will definitely make you feel gross." Dr. H said.

"I guess we'll be admitted." And Natalie didn't sound put out by this development. In fact, Cason thought she sounded almost relieved.

"Yep, that earns you a stay in the hotel." Dr. H began typing up orders. "You can hang out in the treatment area until your room is ready, and then we'll get you settled in. I'll have your nurse go ahead and start fluids and a broad-spectrum antibiotic. And you'll need some more platelets." Dr. H squeezed her shoulder comfortingly. "Let's get you better. Do you need anything for pain? Some of my patients say when they are sick, their phantom pains are worse."

"They're manageable," she sighed. "I think it'll be okay."

"Just tell us what you need, Cason." He smiled at her, all reassurance and confidence. Natalie and Cason moved slowly from the exam area to the fishbowl.

There was Davis again in the middle of the room. Nurses, patients, and parents all bustled around him, but he was all Cason could see.

He was clearing toys from the tables, scrubbing the tables free of crayon, and putting out little tubs of Play-Doh.

He looked tired.

The joy that had filled his eyes and his wonky smile were gone.

She wasn't narcissistic enough to think it was because they had broken up, or whatever. But she did want to know what had taken his joy.

Her nurse settled her into one of the chairs in the curtained-off area. All the private rooms were taken by patients getting treatment. The nurse closed the curtain as Cason got ready for her port to be accessed. Rubbing alcohol and iodine filled her nostrils and the coldness was so sharp that it nearly hurt. There was pressure, and then the prick of the needle moving through her skin and into the device. The taste of saline made her gag as the needle was taped into place. Even months after her diagnosis and chemo treatments, this part was still one of the things that she hated most.

Her fluids were started and the antibiotics ordered. Natalie sat next to her, going over something for the company. Natalie had taken a temporary sabbatical after Cason's surgery, although she still went to work a few hours each week to help the interim director get adjusted. The whole thing still sort of surprised Cason. All it took was an amputation for Cason to become more important than ballet in Natalie's life.

"Mrs. Martin, I know you've said you aren't interested in the parent support group, but my mom wanted me to let you know she was here and that they had lunch. If anything, go grab a sandwich." Davis smiled gently, like he was trying to coax a nervous puppy.

"Do you mind if I go, Cason?"

Cason nearly swallowed her tongue in surprise.

"I'll only go for a bit, just to get a bite," Natalie was quick to say.

"Sure." Her voice was stronger, and she felt mildly better now that the fever was breaking.

"Okay, I'll be back soon." She kissed Cason's head, like she was a little girl and not her once-most-promising ballerina.

"Need anything?" Davis didn't take Natalie's chair like he once would have. He didn't reach for her hand or get any closer. He fussed with the magazines in his hand and shifted his weight.

Cason wanted him to stay with her.

And that shocked her a little.

"How are you?" she asked instead. She pulled herself up a little so she wasn't quite lying down. "Really. Not the answer you'd feed me because you think it's what I need."

His smile-with-a-wink soothed her nerves, and he sat down next to her. "I need a friend."

"It just so happens, I do too."

chapter Thirty-Three

If someone had listened close enough, they would have been able to hear the thumping of Davis's heart. He was standing outside Cason's room. It had been two days since Davis had spoken with her. And they had made tentative steps back into friendship.

Today, he stood there, sort of frozen, afraid to knock.

"Excuse me." One of his old nurses bumped into him as she knocked on the door and entered. There was a smile on her face as she'd done it, clearly letting Davis know he was in the way.

"Great news!" he heard the nurse say to Cason.

"I can go home?" Cason replied. Their voices were muffled through the door. And he shouldn't be listening anyway.

"Not that good." The nurse laughed. "I think I saw Davis loitering around."

"Davis doesn't loiter," Cason laughed. "He's just waiting until you're done before he comes in."

"She's right." He opened the door, just peering his head in. "I'm never quite sure what you're going to do in here."

"Just antibiotics," Cason assured him. "Nothing that requires me to be naked."

The rush of heat that filled his face was instantaneous. He most definitely should not be thinking of Cason Martin naked.

"Remember, her counts are still low." The nurse laughed as she left the room.

"Was she insinuating that I'm germy?" Davis used the sanitizer foam before sitting in the chair close to Cason's bedside.

"I know you're germy." Cason smiled. There was a little awkwardness between them, but it was slowly dissipating. "I'm glad you're here."

"Bored?" He wanted to touch her. The feeling of her soft hands in his was still easy to remember. "Where's your mom?"

"You will never believe me." She laughed, and a brightness lit her eyes, something he hadn't seen since before her surgery. It made the spark of hope in his belly light just a little, like when someone clapped for Tinkerbell in *Peter Pan*. "She's at the parent support group."

Davis smiled right back, the hope starting to glow and pulse more in him. "Well, that is shocking."

"And she asked how you were doing."

"Did you hypnotize her or something?" He leaned forward, wanting to be closer to her. There was an easiness to their talking, even if it didn't quite have the same feeling as before. They were different people now, so instead of resuming what they were, they were beginning something new.

Amazing how in one day everything could change.

"And . . . she wanted to know if I could meet more of your Camp Chemo friends."

"I think Mari, Noah, and Jase might stop by today." A flicker of excitement floated down his sternum and met with the hope. "Next thing you know, she's going to not only agree to you going to camp, but want you to."

"If I'm not mistaken, the director from camp is at the parent support group today talking about it."

"I'd better hide if Margaret is around." He laughed a little. "I'm not always her favorite person."

"Why?" She leaned closer and ducked her head as if they were conspiring.

"I'm a bit of a trouble maker."

"Not you, Davis Channing," Cason laughed. And Davis breathed. He might have still wanted to crawl into the bed with her, hold her, or hell, just hold her hand. But her laughter, her friendship was better than nothing.

"Aren't you supposed to be working around here or something?" Noah walked in, all bright smile and confidence.

"Hiding from Margaret." Davis moved to his friend, giving him a hug. "Noah, this is Cason."

"Margaret's around?" Mari came into the room. "Someone warn Jase."

chapter Thirty-Four

"Is Jase a troublemaker too?" Cason asked as Mari sat down on the bed next to her.

"Her counts are low," Davis warned.

"I'm not too infectious. I showered last week." Mari tucked herself into Cason and stuck her tongue out at Davis. "Jase just ends up in the wrong place at the wrong time," Mari defended.

"I am always innocent." Jase came in, sticking his wallet back in his pocket. "The parking at this place is unreasonable."

"Cry me a river, rich boy." Noah walked around the room, assessing the whole scene. Cason watched the way he moved, watched how he walked, and was fascinated by one fact: she couldn't figure out which of his legs had been amputated. "I'm Noah Edwards." He smiled, white teeth on black skin, and Cason could feel the palpable energy coming off him. "I hear you're a new amp."

"Cason," Mari corrected. "Her name isn't 'Amp.' We are not amputees, we are people with amputations."

"You've been hanging out with Heather again." Noah shifted his weight before lifting one of his legs and doing a calf stretch. She still couldn't tell which leg was a prosthesis.

"Mari's summer research paper is on the benefits of person-first language," Jase explained. He was incredibly handsome. And if it hadn't been so obvious that he was hopelessly in love with Mari, Cason could have seen herself developing a huge crush. He had blond hair, sun-kissed and windblown, with blue eyes that were impossible not to notice.

"AP Psych," Mari shrugged. "What you need to know is you get to identify however you want to."

"So, in other words, if I want to be an amputee, I get to be an amputee." Noah didn't stop moving, he paced the room, like he needed to be running instead of in the cramped space. Where did this energy come from?

"Yeah." Mari shrugged again, knocking Cason with each movement. Cason looked around the room, filled with people—friends, maybe? Had she invited them? Was there a party that she didn't know about? Would she get in trouble for having this many people in her room?

"I figured you were getting bored," Davis explained. He'd been quiet, but there was a happiness in his eyes. "So I invited them up."

"To the Teen Room." Heather waltzed in and out almost immediately, carrying a large bag of something.

Davis helped Cason up, getting her crutches and then pushing her IV pole beside her.

"I'm not here and not handing you these cards or

leaving these snacks," Heather said to the group once they had settled around a table. Noah picked up the stack of Uno cards and began to shuffle. Cason immediately noticed a gleam in his eyes. Davis, without hesitation, got up and began to pass cups to his friends. As he put Cason's cup in front of her, his hand lingered on her shoulder. *He's friendly. We're friends.* But those words didn't explain the tiny shocks running under where his hand had been.

"I'm sorry, do we know you?" Mari teased, taking a handful of popcorn.

"I've closed the Teen Room for a couple hours." Heather explained. "This is the only way you can legally have this stuff in here. Don't pour Coke into the PlayStation." And she swept out, a cape of long, blond hair behind her.

Cason didn't have to say much, everyone around her filled in the gaps in conversation. She finally found out that Noah had his right leg, like her, but she still couldn't tell. There was no hitch in his walk, no wobble to his gate. Hell, he walked better than some of the dancers she knew.

"So, we were racing down the slopes." Mari said. "I was flying."

"But I still won!" Noah interrupted. There was a friendly rivalry between them that Cason instantly noticed.

"You cheated," Mari declared, "but I won in the end. While he was busy gloating, I grabbed his prosthesis from where he'd propped it up against a rock outside the bathrooms and hid it in the girls' room."

"You did not!" Cason laughed. Again, another full-bodied and glorious laugh.

"She totally did." Jase smirked, seemingly used to his girlfriend's antics. He was quiet where she was gregarious. "Noah got her back the next summer at camp, though."

"I still contest that I was innocent of all wrongdoing." Noah held up his hands. "I would never put a fellow camper's name in the drawing for going in the dunk tank."

"Maybe not once, but you would totally put it in there about thirty times," Davis laughed. "This is totally common knowledge."

"Maybe." Noah shrugged, but didn't confirm it or deny it.

"This is a motley crew." Dr. Henderson stepped into the room, eyeing all of them. "Should I expect some sort of glitter outbreak?"

"I have it on good authority that Heather locks it up when Jase and Davis are here together." Mari sipped at her Coke, hiding a smile.

"That is probably for the best." Dr. H stood in the doorway. "Don't tell Cason too many dirty secrets about me. She still thinks I'm a professional."

"Yeah, can we talk about your needle phobia at some point?" Cason laughed.

"Nothing is sacred!" Dr. H laughed on his way down the hall.

"Is he your doc, Cason?" Noah asked.

"He is," she smiled. "Isn't he everyone's?"

"No. I was always jealous of you guys who got him." Jase played a card. "My oncologist retired, but now I go to the long-term survivors' clinic and see a few outside specialists."

"How long have you been off therapy?" Cason picked at the food in front of her.

"Close to eleven years," he smiled. "I had leukemia when I was three."

The conversation never stayed on anything too heavy for too long.

"Have you been fitted yet?" Noah asked Cason as he played a draw four on Mari.

"It's supposed to be next week."

Mari stopped cursing long enough to answer. "It's the weirdest feeling ever."

"Why?" Cason asked. She'd read up on how they fitted a prosthesis.

"It won't be quite as invasive for you because you have some residual limb, but my gynecologist is the only other doc who's gotten quite so familiar with me."

"It's the casting that she's talking about," Noah filled in. "They wrap your residual limb in plaster and let it get hard, like you've broken a bone."

"Or in my case, the right side of my butt," Mari laughed.

Cason was so lost in the conversation, she forgot it

was her turn until Davis took the blue three from her hand and played it for her. "Thanks." She blushed. "Isn't that embarrassing, Mari?"

"Not really, they work really hard to make it as normal as possible." Mari played a draw two for Noah. "But you know, it's new and all of it's just a little weird. If it'll make you feel better, I can come too."

"From the outside, it looks just like any other clinic at the hospital, but there's dust all over and all of these tools that look like instruments of torture," Jase filled in. "When I went with Mari, I couldn't believe it."

Noah explained, "I have a rotationplasty, so they were able to create a knee for me. I couldn't really be an athlete with a limb salvage procedure. If I broke the internal prosthesis, it would mean a major surgery and potentially a full amputation. So this is great, but rotationplasty has its drawbacks," Noah said with a bit of hesitancy. "I mean, my foot is on backward."

Cason had tons of questions. But she didn't want to be rude, she didn't want to pry; hell, she'd just met the guy. Still, they burned in her brain.

"You have to show her," Mari said. The card game had all but stopped, the rest of the table clearly focusing on what was happening. "It's the coolest and weirdest surgery ever."

Noah had no problem rolling up his pant leg, revealing the prosthesis. "The downside is it's really hard to match black skin tone, which is why I went with the Amputee Soccer logo."

"You play, right?" Cason asked lightly, trying not to stare at what she was seeing. Noah undid the Velcro and there it was. His foot was turned completely backward, but attached to his thigh. It was like he had half of a full-sized leg, but his foot was on the wrong way. It still moved and flexed and all the things it should do.

"Yeah." He flexed his foot, massaged it a little.

"Woah." She couldn't help it. It was cool. "Who is your surgeon?"

"Dr. Lee. She's the best." Noah rubbed his foot for another second before putting his prosthesis back into place. "The surgery doesn't always work, sometimes there's blood flow issues."

"Yeah, it was never an option for me," Cason said softly. Would she have danced if it was?

"Dr. Lee did my amputation too," Mari smiled. "I hated her for the first year or so after my surgery."

"Why?" Hearing Mari's confession made Cason feel better about her own feelings toward her own doctor.

"We'd gone to this place in Philly to have a limb salvage done. I picked up an infection sometime between there and here, and the only option was an amputation." She played with Jase's fingers as the conversation turned to her. "I'd spent all this time mentally preparing to have a limb salvage, lots of physical therapy, but I'd still have my leg. I'd look like everyone else." She gave a hapless smile. "Then it failed spectacularly. I was pissed. I mean, I got why it had to be done, but I was still pissed.

"I wasn't concerned about sports, like Noah. I'd wanted to be able to walk, maybe play basketball with my brothers. I mean, I could play wheelchair basketball and maybe, finally, be better than them."

"Her two oldest brothers play for Georgia Tech," Davis explained. "She's never going to be that good."

"True." Mari sipped her soda. "But I can dream."

"Are you still angry at Dr. Lee?" Cason asked.

Mari was quiet for a moment, seeming to be searching within herself. "That's hard." She pursed her lips. "I'm not going to say there aren't times I wish, desperately, that I had two legs. Jase's prom this year, for example. It would have been nice to pick any dress I wanted, and not worry if it was going to cling to where my leg used to be. But I don't hate Dr. Lee the way I did. God, this is going to sound cliché and I hate being a cliché, but I really like being alive." She shrugged. "And to stay alive I get to have one leg."

chapter Thirty-Five

The party broke up when Cason's nurse needed her back in her room for a dose of her antibiotic. Mari hugged her goodbye, with a promise to see her next week. Davis let the feelings of happiness and contentment wash over him. The spark of hope that had bubbled inside him turned warm, glowed, and he felt nearly normal again for the first time since Alexis died.

But...

The addiction pleaded in the back of his brain, begging to be coaxed out, to be massaged and fed until it took over every aspect of his mind. He coughed over the feelings, trying to disrupt them into behaving.

"Coffee?" Jase asked, coming up beside Davis in the hallway outside Cason's room. "Mari's hanging out with Heather for a little longer."

"Sure, let me just check in at home." Davis texted his mom quickly as they moved toward the elevator bank. "Thanks for coming today."

"Cason seems to be in a little better place," Jase said. "When Mari went to see her, she said she was a wreck."

"She didn't just lose her leg, you know? She lost who

she was." Davis shoved his hands in his pockets, keeping his nervous energy contained.

"Yeah, because I was younger, it wasn't like I'd been planning on becoming a serious athlete." Noah led them off the elevator toward the parking lot. "I didn't lose a career." They all piled into Jase's luxury SUV, and Jase began easily navigating the streets of Atlanta.

"You certainly wouldn't be the all-star on the amputee soccer team if you had two legs." Davis laughed lightly. "But, for her, I mean, Cason didn't even go to school full time. She was on her way to New York."

"I'd be a wreck too," Jase admitted slowly. "I can't begin to understand what it's like to have cancer now. I barely remember my own treatments." Jase pulled into a disabled parking spot, taking Noah's placard and hanging it in the window.

"Excuse me, son, but you can't park there," Said a guy, about fifty with a white, wrinkly face and enough confidence that authority oozed out of him.

"We have the designated placard," Jase defended. Davis ground his teeth together, doing everything he could to stop the torrent of words from flowing.

"You can't use your grandpa's sticker just to get better parking."

"It's not my grandfather's, sir." Noah spoke firmly, but not accusingly. "It's mine."

"You three are perfectly fine." Nothing was going to

make this jerk back down. "You are taking this spot from someone who really needs it."

"We don't have to justify our right to park in this space." Davis couldn't keep the words in. He didn't want to talk over Noah, but this guy was working on Davis's last, very-frayed nerve. "We have the proper documentation, and that is what's needed."

"I'm going to call the police."

"You do that." Noah spoke, but never offered to show the guy his prosthesis or even offer an explanation. "And you're going to feel like the world's biggest tool."

"Not all disabilities are visible," Jase muttered as he passed the jerk and they filed into the Daily Grind.

"What a dumbass." Davis was still reeling from the way the guy had drilled them, refusing to let it go.

"My mom went over with me how I should react to this kind of thing when I started driving. That it's better to be polite and firm, but that I don't have to prove anything." Noah sighed. "And it's always some old white dude. Always."

"Is that why you didn't show him your prosthesis?"

"Yeah, it's no one's business but mine." He looked at Davis.

"It's such bullshit." Davis still simmered. "You've been through enough."

"Everyone has a story, Davis. Mine is just more visible . . . sometimes. Jerks like him see me, you know, black and a teenager, and I get called out immediately. You can never be young and disabled, forget being black, young, and disabled. It's like it blows people's minds."

They sat at one of the tables near the window, which gave them a chance to watch the guy who had harassed them.

"We have a placard. We don't owe anyone an explanation." Jase sounded like his attorney father. "I hope he does call the cops."

"He's probably thinking about keying your car." Noah laughed a little, but his normal mirth was missing.

"Does this happen with Mari?" Davis asked. Of course he was thinking of Cason. Would this type of thing happen to her?

"Until she gets out of the car." Jase smiled. "But then people backpedal incredibly hard and talk about what an inspiration she is."

"Seriously?" Davis could picture Mari rolling her eyes at every single person who did that to her.

"It's different for Mari since she doesn't wear a prosthesis." Noah tapped his long fingers on the tabletop, making the napkin confetti Davis had made bounce with each pulse. "I really only hear how inspiring I am if I talk about my cancer or when I'm playing. The second we do something that abled-bodied people feel like we shouldn't be able to do, even if it's just like, walking down stairs or some shit, then we're inspiring."

"Until you're disabled, you can't imagine life being that way, I guess," Jase reasoned. "I know that Mari now refuses to acknowledge people when they say something to her. Or she'll just nod, but she doesn't engage."

"We've talked about it before," Noah said. "We deal with things a little differently, but our lives and amputations are different. I can easily hide as one of you jokers until I take off my prosthesis."

There was a pause. Davis was still trying to keep his rage in check. He briefly thought about calling Detective Avery and having him come up, just to teach the asshat a lesson.

"How are you?" Jase's words jerked Davis out of his thoughts. His friend looked at him with a friendly smile, and the earnestness in his question spoke volumes in only three words.

"It's been tough." Davis thought through his response slowly, tasting each word as he spoke. "John gave me some hard stuff to work on. But honestly, man, there are days that just getting up and not using is all I can do." He admitted it slowly, the words painful in his throat. "I know that it's not what I really want to do. I know that I want to stay sober and that I like where my life is, but also knowing how easy the high is . . ."

"Easy would be nice sometimes." Jase sipped his coffee slowly. "Ever feel like our lives are never easy? Like somehow having cancer has put a black mark over us and we never get to have easy?"

Davis thought about Jase's words. Jase was the most typical cancer kid in the history of cancer kids. He didn't have any outward signs that he'd ever been sick or on intense rounds of chemotherapy. No major physical wounds to show for his battle. But, like all of them, there were psychological wounds, internal wounds. And maybe that was just as debilitating at times.

"Maybe." Davis continued shredding his napkin. "But I think that everyone is probably looking for easy. I mean, Alexis was looking for easy and she didn't have cancer." It was the first time he'd really talked about Alexis with anyone who wasn't in recovery with him. "Ethan is still looking for easy."

"Easy is boring," Noah said. "Everyone can do easy, it's a lot more rewarding to do hard."

"Did you read that on a poster?" Jase laughed at Noah. "Were you on it doing one of your fancy kicks?" The group dissolved into laughter.

But that evening, in his room, Davis thought about those words. He wasn't sure if this hard work was rewarding, but he did know he liked being sober.

chapter Thirty-Six

Cason was tied to the ceiling. Literally. She was wrapped in a soft cotton stocking that went up over her residual limb and nearly under her armpits. Then the prosthetist, the person who would make her leg, had tied more fabric from special hooks in the ceiling and connected it to the soft stocking.

"This will help you stay lateral," Dr. Frankenstein—as she referred to him—explained.

"But you can't swing from it." Mari didn't even look up from her phone as she spoke. "Trust me."

"Mari, you have a prosthesis?" Natalie was sitting in the room with them. Her shoulders were hunched and Cason noted that she looked terrified, or like she was going to drip snotty tears any moment.

"I've had a couple," Mari softened her words, seeming to understand that Mrs. Martin needed a gentle touch right now. "Sometimes I get an itch to try out the new technology and I'll get a new prosthesis."

"But you don't use it?"

"No. But Cason has a residual limb and that'll make it much easier for her." She continued to relieve Natalie's fears. "I'm really the outlier in the group by not wearing my prosthesis, something Noah used to remind me of constantly."

"He has the partial amputation, right?" asked Natalie. Cason watched her mother taking notes, taking in everything Dr. Frankenstein was doing. She had even been attending the parent support groups more regularly.

"Yeah, the rotationplasty," Mari said.

The prosthetist came back in carrying a basin filled with water and several rolls of plaster. He began to unwrap them and then dropped one of them in the water.

"We're doing a traditional casting on Cason instead of using the laser because we want this first socket to be as close to a perfect fit as we can." He began to wrap the plaster around her residual limb, like he was putting a cast on a broken bone. "When you get your final leg, we might do the laser because we'll have a better idea of where your sensitive spots are and where you might get skin breakdown."

Cason held onto the walker that had been placed around her for balance. Mari continued to talk to her mom, but she didn't hear much of it. She watched the way the prosthetist worked his hands over her body, molding the plaster to her, getting it as close to the shape of her residual limb as he could. He excused himself, saying he'd be back in about ten minutes after it had hardened. It was warm, bordering on hot, in the cast. Not uncomfortable except for the fact that it was tight.

She wished she could watch this from outside her body.

She wished it wasn't her body.

Cason knew that her amputation had probably saved her life.

She knew that.

But it didn't make it any easier.

It didn't make her heart break any less, tearing new stitches in the organ each time she looked down and saw what remained of her leg.

And God, she wanted to dance.

"Cason?" Mari pulled her out of the trance. There was a kindness in Mari's voice, it was like she knew, like she understood with just the silence what Cason was feeling and how her life was crumbling right under her. And how right now, she wanted to be anywhere else.

"Are you alright? Is it too tight?" Natalie turned into a Mama Bear, instantly ready to rip into Dr. F.

"No." The word was thick with tears that were setting on her heart, pressing on the new stitches, plucking each one, until they popped. "It's just . . . this is my life now. Hanging from this contraption is the closest I'm going to get to dancing again."

"Oh, Cason." Natalie's voice broke over her name and tears slid down her elegant face. And for the millionth time in the seven weeks that Cason had been an amputee, her mom wrapped her arms around her, and they wept. It was full of bitter tears and crushed dreams.

Dreams that had been so close to happening.

~

The tears had dried and Cason was still strung up to the ceiling. The room was a large exam room, but seemed to have a casing of dust over any uncovered surface. A set of even parallel bars was against one wall, there was an exam table, and then the place where Cason was now tethered to the ceiling. "It's a good look." Kelsey, the physical therapist from hell, had come into the fitting room just after Cason and Natalie finished weeping. Cason wasn't positive, but she was pretty sure Mari went and got her. "And it's got me thinking." Kelsey circled around Cason, tugging ever so slightly at the cotton fabric that held Cason lateral.

"About your next torture session?" Cason had no snark in her voice, she was completely serious. Kelsey was not her favorite person on the planet despite what both Noah and Mari said.

"Well, sort of." She walked around Cason, all fluid and grace, reminding Cason of how she faltered and walked like a baby elephant. Kelsey fingered the straps holding Cason up to the ceiling.

Dr. F came back in and sat in front of Cason. "Are you here bothering the patients?" There was a friendly camaraderie between the prosthetist and physical therapist. And Cason thought she might hate both of them.

"I was just saying to Cason that I think we're going

to try some new stuff." Kelsey had a gleam in her dark-brown eyes that Cason did not like. "It'll definitely help you build your abdominal muscles, get your core back into shape, and we can work on that upper body strength that you've been using on your crutches."

"What exactly are you thinking?" Natalie seemed more intrigued than Cason. Then again, Natalie really liked Kelsey if for no other reason than she would help Cason walk again.

"Oh, this is going to be good," Mari laughed. "Whenever Kelsey gets this look in her eye, you know she has big plans."

"Kelsey, I'm still on treatment. I'm not exactly up for big plans." Cason wanted nothing to do with any of Kelsey's plans.

The next words that Kelsey said stopped all the air in the room.

"What if I said you were going to dance again?"

chapter Thirty-Seven

The Daily Grind was busy, and Davis had a pit of guilt in his stomach because he wasn't working that day. People sat and chatted, all of them seeming to be having a good time, which just made Davis hate what he was about to do even more.

His phone rang, and automatically, he wondered if it was Cason, but the number on the screen made his throat close with nerves. Davis debated for a moment about sending it to his voicemail, not having the energy to deal with this too. Instead, he answered, holding the phone in his sweaty hand against his ear.

"Davis?" It was Detective Avery. And just the sound of the man's voice made Davis's blood thicken. His blood slugged through his arteries and veins, pulsing and nearly making it impossible for Davis to hear what the detective was calling to say.

"We picked up Ethan last night."

Those words signaled a release so strong in Davis's system that he had to sit down on one of the stools at the counter of the Daily Grind. His legs no longer worked the way they were supposed to, they could no longer hold him up, his circulatory system had apparently forgotten about the appendages.

"Okay," Davis heard himself answer. "What does this mean?"

"He was arraigned this morning and then released on bail." The small moment of relief was dashed in that one sentence. "Try not to worry. We still have the protection order, and if Ethan breaks the TPO, it's back to jail, and his parents lose the bond they posted for him."

"Right." But right now, Davis was less concerned about Ethan finding him.

Davis was much more concerned about the possibility of him finding Ethan.

He wasn't sure he'd actually said goodbye. Davis had a hard time thinking about anything other than what he was doing.

He was starting to hate it here. It had become a place of difficult and painful conversations. And, to be honest, he was way over having them. But here he sat, waiting on Alexis Foster's parents.

They entered the shop, and he immediately noticed just how worn they looked, like the world was pressing on their chests and neither of them could take in a full breath without it choking them. Mrs. Foster had the same curly hair that Alexis had. And Mr. Foster had the bright eyes of his daughter. Davis felt so much guilt for being the reason she wasn't here.

"Thanks for meeting me," he finally said. The words

hurt his throat and built a hard knot at the base of his neck. It was hard to breathe.

"It's nice to see you, Davis." Mrs. Foster was kind. He didn't deserve her kindness. Mr. Foster didn't say anything: tight lines around his lips, pinched eyes; he was only there because Mrs. Foster had made him come.

"I have been struggling in my own recovery." He said the words for the first time aloud. He hadn't wanted to admit that the pull to use, the snake that lived in his stomach, was constantly calling for the taste and feel of a high.

"I'm sorry to hear that," Mrs. Foster said, all grace and tact.

"Why are we here?" Mr. Foster asked, all resentment and sadness.

"One of the steps is about asking for forgiveness." He paused, finding words and courage. "I should have asked you for forgiveness a long time ago." Thickness filled his words and the knot pushed at his own tears. God, he was a mess. "And I, in no way, deserve any graciousness you show me."

"Damn right," Mr. Foster spit. "You should still be in jail. If you'd been locked up where you should have been, Alexis would be clean."

"Robert," Mrs. Foster soothed, "Alexis had every opportunity to get well."

Davis let them speak, their words and silences saying everything that could never be said. And Davis stopped wiping at his tears. He didn't make excuses for himself, he couldn't. Because what Mr. Foster was saying, the hatefulness in his voice, was the same voice that filled Davis's own mind.

"You don't need to accept my apology," Davis paused, scrubbing at his face. "In fact, I wouldn't accept it, if I were you. But I'm here and I'm offering. I won't make platitudes or promises about living my life for Alexis, because I can't. I can only live my life for myself. But I will work tirelessly to stay sober and not to hurt anyone else."

Neither of her parents said anything. Mrs. Foster nodded, a weak smile trembling on her lips. Maybe pleased? Mr. Foster no longer looked like he wanted to kill Davis, but the sadness, the undeniable sadness of losing a child, seemed to fill every wrinkle on his face. And Davis knew that it was all his fault.

After that, they had nothing else to say to each other. The Fosters left, and Davis sat at the same table he'd been at not that long ago with Mr. Williams. He unfolded the list, staring at it, remembering why he fought so hard to stay clean and sober. Remembering why it was important.

But addiction was powerful. And his heart was so hurt. His body ached to find a release.

To find something. Find someone.

Before he knew it, he was out the door of the café.

chapter Thirty-Eight

She didn't remember the first time she walked into a dance studio, but her earliest memories were of standing at the *barre*. She hadn't been quite tall enough to reach it, but stood behind the ballerinas and moved through the positions. Not in a toddler class or a mommy-and-me class, but with the professional ballerinas of her mother's company.

There was no doubt that Cason would always remember the first time she stepped into an aerial studio.

It was a converted church just east of downtown Atlanta. It had high, vaulted ceilings with beams arching across them, reinforced to support the rainbow of silks and trapezes that hung there.

"I can see why my prosthetic fitting made her think of this place," Cason said to her mom.

"Hey there," Kelsey greeted them. "Thanks for agreeing to move your therapy here today."

"What exactly are you thinking for Cason?" Natalie eyed all the equipment with suspicion. "And how will this help prepare her for her prosthesis?"

"You've lost a lot of muscle from the chemo and just

being sick." Kelsey walked them both over toward one of the long, purple silks, letting it slip between her fingers. "And I think we could start to build it all back up with these. Cason's going to need some new muscles to use her prosthesis and her core needs to be redeveloped. I think by working on the silks, we can accomplish a lot of that.

"It won't replace what you've lost, Cason. I know that." Kelsey squeezed Cason's arm softly, comfortingly. "And you could hate it, but I'd never forgive myself if we didn't try."

Each pulse tingled in Cason's neck. Her hands gripped her crutches, sweating now with anticipation, and she could hear the blood rushing in her ears.

She nodded. "Let's try it." Cason turned to her mother and smiled reassuringly.

"I'll leave you two to it," Natalie said as she left. Cason studied the silks, the mixture of potential and disaster twined into her heartbeat.

Kelsey wrapped one of the silks around Cason's wrist, tightening it until the silk could support her weight. Cason watched, nerves sliding in her belly. Her sweaty palms gripped the silk, feeling the softness turn into strength.

And Cason pulled up.

It was an unconscious thought and internal need. Cason was doing nothing more than holding her body up with her arms, but it was the way it made her heart move, made her spine straighten. It was more than a simple movement.

Instantly, her toe, just inches off the mat-covered floor, went into a point.

With each movement Cason was able to accomplish, they celebrated. She was happy to see that her body still remembered how to move with the gracefulness of a ballerina, that her long-forgotten strength was still there.

"I don't want you to go too high, but I think if we spend some more serious time here that this could really be something."

By the end of the hour, her stomach muscles burned the way they had before she'd gotten cancer. Like they had after the best rehearsals, where her toes were bleeding and her muscles ached from doing the extraordinary.

But Cason didn't feel like she'd done much of anything extraordinary today.

Perspiration made her top sticky, and she wished she'd thought to wear a sweatband around her head. No eyebrows or eyelashes meant that sweat could easily drip down her face and into her eyes, which sort of sucked when you were trying to climb into a silk.

She had barely managed to pull herself up into the hanging ribbons, her body was so tired and all her muscles dormant. Kelsey was writing things down, making notes, and only sort of riding Cason like a ballet master.

"So next week, we'll meet at the hospital twice and here twice," Kelsey noted. "You don't have treatment then, which means your counts will still be good. You'll have to have decent platelets to go up in the silks." She was rattling off things. "But, if we can do two days of strength training and two days of this, I think you'll not only start seeing improvement in your abilities, but you'll also start to feel better. You're an athlete, Cason, and it's time to start treating your body like that again."

"Tell that to the chemo," she sighed. But there was a strange thrill in her.

It had been hard. Hard in the way that she'd missed. Climbing even just a foot or two off the ground had been exhilarating.

And she wanted to do it again.

chapter Thirty-nine

A fine layer of grime covered everything. The smells of putrid toilet water, rust, and iron all melded together. It was the scent all crappy public bathrooms had. Sweat slowly trickled down his neck and he waited.

Waited.

It's a quick fix.

One high.

In his mind, he could taste the chemicals filling his mouth, burning his lungs, and numbing his brain. His hands shook as he ran them under the faucet, letting unclean water purify him.

Davis's throat closed as he thought of holding a pipe in his hand, the way the smoke would curl around his nose, the pull of it into his lungs. He wanted to feel that, to feel the high as it comforted and filled every crevice in his worn body.

The bathroom door opened.

"Davis." Ethan's face stretched around his perfectly straight teeth in fake surprise. "Long time no see."

"Do you have it?" Nausea filled his throat and blood pounded at his temples.

"What are you looking for?" Ethan leaned against the door, effectively closing them both in the small room. "How about your usual?" Ethan put a hand in his pocket, pulling at something.

Davis's brain screamed.

Pleaded.

Begged.

Just one! Just one! Fix me!

"I guess it's good I got out on bond," another smile, "and that TPO's are just a piece of paper." Another reminder that Ethan could have killed Davis.

That he still might.

"This one's on me, part of the customer loyalty program." Ethan reached out to shake his hand and Davis felt him pass the small bag with the three pills in it. "It's good to have you back."

There it was.

Davis's mouth went dry. His breath stuck in the pockets of his lungs, refusing to do the work his body needed.

"Later." Ethan flushed the toilet in the broken stall, walking out of the dank bathroom. Davis was alone. The dope in his hand. He could feel each pill in the pocket, feel the round edges, the numbers stamped on them. He could feel himself grinding it up, deciding which way he wanted to get his high. Smoke it? Find a needle? That'd be easy enough.

It would feel so good.

Sweat dripped down the side of his face, his blood

raced, and his mind filled with words and feelings. His endorphins rushed through him, making the dope he held firmly in his hands tremble with his shaking.

Just one fix.

Just one.

chapter Forty

He was gross.

Sitting on the floor in any public bathroom was disgusting, but this one, one where a drug deal had just gone down, was vile.

In his hand was the baggie. Three little pills. Pills that had been produced to take pain away.

They will take all your pain away. He'd said those words to Alexis.

And they had.

Gagging, he spit on the floor, uncaring, as if he could spit out the urge to use.

His phone rang.

He hated his phone.

It'd only been used for bad stuff lately.

Cason's fall.

Calling Ethan.

He answered the phone blindly and held it to his ear, ready to get whomever it was off the phone as quickly as he could.

"Davis?" He didn't immediately recognize the voice

on the other end. "This is Margaret, the director from Camp Chemo."

He gripped the little bag of pills tighter in his hand. He was squeezing so hard he was sure he could feel the serial numbers branding his skin.

"Hi, Margaret." He should have made a joke. He should have said something about how whatever prank had been pulled, it was not his fault, that he hadn't even been at camp last year. Since she was in charge of camp, it was often her job to find out what chaos he'd caused.

"We just had our staff training, and I wanted to let you know that we would like you to be the one to light the first campfire this year."

His heart stopped.

His mouth was painfully dry.

And his heart hurt. He wasn't sure whether it was squeezing any blood through his body, because Davis was sure it had stopped beating after Margaret spoke.

Being the person to light the first campfire was an honor, something reserved for campers that were respected by counselors and campers alike.

"Me?" He choked on the words. He couldn't be that person. He had dope in his hands.

In his hands.

"Yes, Davis." He could hear her smile. "Everyone is so proud of you."

"But . . . I'm . . ." Tears and snot slid down his face.

There was nothing pretty about any of this. It was all gross and disgusting and vile. "I'm such a joke."

"No, Davis. You are a fighter." There might have been tears in Margaret's voice. "And that's what Camp Chemo is about."

"Oh, God." The words whispered but they wanted to rip. "Are you sure?"

"I was a little afraid you might try to convince the camp to leave a trail of glitter, but I think it's perfect."

His laugh turned into a sob. Davis pulled himself together just long enough to say thanks and hang up the phone.

He sat there and stared at the pills in his hands.

Launching himself off the ground, he vomited everything in his stomach into the toilet. He heaved and sobbed all at once. He hadn't used, but it was like his stomach was reacting to the overwhelming feelings that moved through him.

He flushed.

He wiped his face with the stale, brown paper towel off the roll.

He stared in the mirror.

And before he thought too much about it, he opened the small packet with the dope and dumped them into the toilet he'd vomited in.

He flushed and watched as the pills circled. His stomach was still in knots. He briefly thought about chasing them, about scooping them up from the toilet water and seeing if it was at all possible to get high.

But then, he'd hear Margaret's words.

And for this moment, he was sober.

chapter Forty-one

Natalie stood as Cason crutched back into the lobby of the aerial studio, having just finished her PT for the day. Cason was sticky with sweat, and her calf-length pants clung to her leg and residual limb. She'd tucked up the extra length of the pants into the back like she'd seen Mari do, but she was seriously thinking of just cutting them off. She wore a tank top, not able to fathom slipping on a leotard right now. But there was no strict dress code at the aerial studio like there had been at the ABC.

"How did it go?" Natalie put an arm around Cason, not seeming to care that she was damp with sweat. "Kelsey said I can't watch yet."

"It's tough." Cason could already feel her muscles protesting as she took small steps on her crutches. "But a good tough."

"Like when you worked on that *pirouette* combination for the piece Markov did for you."

A small smile of a memory appeared on Cason's lips. "I didn't know you knew about that." They were in the car now, driving out of the quaint neighborhood toward the interstate.

"I knew how hard you were working on it." Natalie was relaxed, even her hair was down. The summer seemed to agree with her. "Chemo next week."

"Ugh." Cason would have rather talked about dance, even if it was painful, than the idea of chemo. "At least it's only the one day."

"But it's a brutal one day." Natalie seemed just as put out as Cason was. And she didn't even have to have the chemo, just participate in the cleanup.

There was silence in the car, but it wasn't uncomfortable. Just quiet, as both women were thinking different things. Cason thought about the piece that Markov, her mother's favorite contemporary choreographer, had made just for her. It was one that she had only had the privilege of dancing in public twice, once for a benefit for the ABC and the fated audition for the Studio Company.

"Mom, how are the residential camps going?" The ABC had camps all summer for advanced students. Natalie used it as a place to look for potential students that she might want to offer places in the company. It was one of the best recruiting tools she had.

"I'm not actually sure. I've got Denise handling everything." They drove up the connector toward midtown from downtown Atlanta. Cason watched as buildings and landmarks passed by, but was doing her best to keep her face casual. Her mother never gave up that kind of control.

"Oh, really?"

"Yeah, I've been meaning to talk to you about some

things." Natalie glanced at Cason, clearly a little nervous. "My sabbatical from the ABC is going to be longer . . . and maybe not even temporary."

Cason listened to her mother's words. She had to process them, letting each word roll around her head. She had to break them down by the syllable to remember what they meant. "Really?"

"Yes." Traffic was moving for once, which meant Cason could look at her mother while Natalie had to focus on the road ahead. "Don't be so surprised." Natalie lightened her voice, but the tightness around her lips gave her away.

"Mom, why? The hard stuff is over." Cason tried to find the right words. "I mean, my surgery is done."

"You know I've been talking to Dr. Kelly and going to the parent support group."

Both of those things still shocked Cason. "Yes."

"And some of the parents in the support group helped me see that you, not ballet, are my job. And you have cancer."

Cason was quiet. Her head was filled with words that couldn't come together to form sentences, and her heart hurt a little. But mostly, there was relief. Finally, she wasn't the only one carrying this load. She wasn't the one that oversaw getting better and dancing again.

"I need to be able to take you to appointments and physical therapy. You still have about six months of chemo. And until you can drive again, you'll need me. And then, there are things I can do for other moms like me."

They pulled into the driveway of their house. Natalie put the car in park and looked at Cason with her blue eyes. Eyes that were just a little fuzzy with tears.

"Mom, I'll always need you." Cason sniffed hard, fighting her own fuzzy eyes. "Who else is going to help me find new dreams?"

Natalie let a tear drift down her cheek, not bothering to wipe it or even check her makeup. "Cason, you have always found your own way, and thanks to therapy and people who've been there before me, I know you will again."

"I guess that pamphlet on the parental support group Davis gave you wasn't a complete waste of paper." Cason sniffed again, but no longer fought the tears on her cheeks.

"Yeah, shockingly, the person who has been through it all before knew just what he was talking about." Natalie's wry smile wobbled. "And I know that I was not exactly warm toward him."

"It's safe to say you were a bitch." For a minute, Cason thought that Natalie was going to lay into her for swearing, something that months ago—hell, weeks ago—she would have done. But instead, a peal of laughter broke the emotional moment between them.

"I was," Natalie agreed, opening her door and climbing out of the car. She helped Cason out, holding her close for a minute. "And I was wrong about how cancer was going to change us."

Cason buried her face in the crook her mother's neck, inhaling the scent that was only hers: gardenia and peppermint.

She breathed.

She had a mom and not just an artistic director.

chapter Forty-Two

Physical therapy was her least favorite thing in the world. Her muscles were weak, and now the simplest of movements ached. She stood on her one leg, correcting her balance by touching the mirrored wall. She had to move her leg in the center of her body. All she could think was how strange it looked.

Cason had been back to the aerial studio three more times, but was currently in the PT suite at the hospital. Her platelets were too low to allow her to dangle from silks even if she was barely two feet off the floor.

"You need to figure out how you're going to carry a tray at school," Kelsey said, bringing Cason back to the task at hand, which was just simple balance.

"Uh, I'll bring my lunch." Cason thrust her arms out to keep her balance and Kelsey grabbed the support band around her waist.

"What about college?" Kelsey questioned. They locked eyes in the mirror as Cason righted herself. "It's not that far off. Let's get you stretching."

Cason lay on the floor, her foot strapped into a stretchy band, and worked on flexing, building back some of the muscle she'd lost. There were other kids working in the therapy room today: some babies with helmets on, kids who used walkers or crutches like hers, and they were all playing. This was hard work, and no amount of bubbles being blown or balls for her to kick would convince her this was playtime.

Kelsey grabbed one of the big fitness balls and rolled it over to where Cason was on the floor. "I want you to balance on the ball, and then I'm going to add some weights."

Cason groaned and balanced herself on the large exercise ball. Once she was centered, her residual limb rested on the ball next to her full thigh. She had been fitted for her test socket earlier this week, and seeing her residual limb encased in hard plastic was something she was going to have to get used to. It didn't matter that Dr. Frankenstein reminded her that the official socket wouldn't be as hard as the test one, she would still have plastic around her leg. This was her new normal.

"Are you going to Camp Chemo?" Kelsey pushed her to do more, find her balance.

"It's on my calendar." She straightened her posture, attempting to find her center and roll her tail bone down. And promptly lost her balance.

Kelsey smiled, helped her straighten and realign, then stepped back. "I'll be there."

"So, you're telling me I can't escape your torture sessions even then, huh?"

They moved from the ball to the floor, Cason on her back. "I teach yoga and dance." Kelsey pulled back on Cason's foot, stretching her heel, pulling at muscles in her calf. It felt so good and familiar that Cason nearly groaned.

"Of course you do."

"I'm going to suggest something and I don't want you to immediately shoot me down."

"What?" Cason was now completely prepared to shut her down.

"I want you to think about performing on the silks at camp."

"That's ridiculous." Cason forgot all about how she wasn't supposed to shoot her down instantly. "I can barely get into them."

"You weren't supposed to shoot me down immediately," Kelsey teased. "We've still got some time, and I think we could up our sessions at the studio versus here. Just think about it."

"Okay." But Cason already knew she wasn't going to do that. She wasn't going to be some sideshow so the people at this camp could feel good about helping poor sick children. She had been a professional ballerina and she would not be something to inspire people.

She wasn't going to perform again.

Ever.

chapter Forty-Three

In just a few hours, Davis would be leaving for camp. The anticipation was so charged in his body that he practically vibrated. Sitting on his hands, he listened as the meeting chairperson thanked the speaker at the NA meeting that morning.

Maybe he was also nervous about this.

Since scoring from Ethan two weeks ago, Davis was back going to meetings daily. He hadn't spoken publically about what had happened, except to call Detective Avery and tell him. Davis hadn't been shocked when his probation officer had called and asked for a surprise drug test.

And even though Davis knew that he hadn't used, his stomach had been cinched in knots as he waited for the results.

The all-clear was one of the best moments of his life.

"Before we dismiss, we have a celebration." There was John, speaking at the podium. Davis hadn't even known he was there, but now heat flooded his face. "Davis Channing is getting ready to leave for camp, and will be gone on his one-year sober date. But before he leaves, I thought we could celebrate with him." He motioned for Davis to come to the front and stand with him. Davis moved, his feet shuffling, and he stared at the floor, unable to look at the others scattered around the Saturday morning meeting.

"I am proud of the progress you've made." There might have been tears in John's eyes as he spoke. "I remember watching as you spiraled down, but seeing where you are now is a blessing." John held the chip out and then put it in Davis's hand, closing his fingers around it. "You've worked hard to get here, and I cannot wait to see where you go."

The weight of the chip in his hand felt like every moment that Davis had been able to choose sobriety all in one small object. He stared at the grooves and indentions, the insignias, and logos, memorizing it. "Thanks." The word was thick in his mouth and Davis was surprised by the knot in his throat. "There were days I wasn't sure I was going to see this." He looked at John as he spoke. The ache of a confession sat on the back of his tongue, pricking his throat with words.

"I called my old dealer. I scored." The words hurt his throat, they filled the excess in his body, and anything that wasn't full of blood and cells was filled with the sorrow and frustration of his past. "I scored and was ready to use again." He coughed to clear his throat, but it didn't work, the only thing that happened was more and more tears. "But miracles happen, and I got one that day. I got news that reminded me why I wanted to be sober, why being sober was important." Feeling brave, Davis looked out at the small crowd. "I flushed it."

He might have said more and John might have said more, but Davis couldn't hear it. All he could hear was the blood whooshing in his ears. All he could feel was the wonderful weight of that chip.

He was sober.

~

Cason [4:30PM]: I'm nervous.

So was he, and not at all for the same reasons that Cason was. Davis was waiting for his mom outside his meeting. They were leaving straight from the meeting to go to camp. He was going to be a little late, everyone else was already on their way; but he'd needed to go to that meeting. He felt so much better having confessed.

And he had a one-year chip in his hand.

Davis [4:32PM]: You'll be fine. You know everyone.

Cason [4:37PM]: Not EVERYONE. Besides what if I'm not with Mari?

Davis [4:39PM]: Heather is your counselor. I saw her list the other day while I was cleaning.

"That was really nice of you to talk about me in your meeting." Vomit filled Davis's throat. The voice was familiar, and one he had hoped to never hear again. He had to stop texting Cason after meetings.

"Ethan," Davis managed to say.

"I thought you might need a boost." He appraised Davis.

But Davis wasn't trapped this time. It was broad daylight, and there were people milling about. Without thinking too much about it, he walked down the steps, past Ethan. "I'm fine."

"I heard you flushed my gift." Ethan followed, coming up close, grabbing Davis by the arm. "That's rude."

"Let me go." Davis pulled, but Ethan's hold only tightened.

"Remember what happened to Alexis." Ethan's fingers dug into Davis's skin. "I don't like it when people don't pay."

Davis stared right at Ethan. And for the first time, Davis had some power. He wasn't meeting his own dangerous needs or needing something from Ethan. Ethan needed something from him.

"Yeah, and I also remember that you are breaking that TPO." Davis didn't back down because he knew that Ethan couldn't hurt him right now. "But it's just a piece of paper."

"Last time I didn't kill you." The words were harsh, full of anger and outrage, but their low volume reminded Davis of a bad made-for-TV-movie. "Next time you won't be so lucky."

Ethan didn't hit him or even touch Davis as he bounded down the rest of the steps and into the park. Within thirty seconds, Davis began to shake, his body reacting to everything that happened in such a short moment. Fuzz filled his brain and his knees wanted him to sink down, but he couldn't because Ethan could come back. With fingers that shook, he dialed the emergency number Detective Avery gave him.

"Detective Avery?" Davis's voice wobbled and he hated it. "Ethan found me outside my NA meeting and threatened me."

The conversation was over. It was quick. Just facts and Detective Avery making promises.

For once, Davis believed him.

chapter Forty-Four

There was a smell to camp. Maybe it was part of the heat of Georgia summer or the fact that they were miles away from the city. Or maybe it was just the calmness that camp meant to him. Since the first time he'd set foot on the soil five years ago, he'd been at peace here.

This was still true.

Davis breathed in, letting the heat and humidity fill him. If he closed his eyes, he could still see everything around him; it was ingrained in his heart.

And he felt safe. He knew Ethan couldn't find him here.

"Davis," Margaret smiled, greeting him with a warm hug. "Welcome home."

"Thanks." His parents were off to the side, unloading his stuff and making sure it was taken to his cabin. "It's great to be back."

"Are you ready for tonight?" She put her arm around him, and her dark braids brushed his arm. "I got the craft sticks you asked for."

"Thanks for going along with it." He still couldn't quite believe he was going to be opening camp this year.

That he had been chosen for this honor despite being an addict helped him realize that his addiction didn't define him. It was just one of his layers.

"I think it's a great idea. Maybe we'll incorporate it into all of our first campfires from now on." Margaret squeezed him like he was still thirteen. She had a warm face, long, black box braids, and dark eyes. Margaret could comfort or scare the hell out of you with just one look. And Davis had been on the receiving end of both.

"You're all set." His dad came over to them. "I wish we could stay to see you tonight."

"You totally cannot." Davis shook his head. "I've been waiting for this week for over a year."

"We know." His mom smiled and hugged him, holding him close, tucking his head just under her chin. "I am so proud of you."

"Thanks, Mama." He wouldn't cry. Not right now.

"You have done great work this year, Davis." His dad hugged him and he was instantly a six-year-old again. Or maybe a thirteen-year-old who had just been diagnosed with lymphoma. Either way, his parents still loved him. No matter how hard he'd pushed at them.

"We'll see you on Saturday." His mom kissed his cheek and then they were gone. And Davis had the whole week.

"Dinner is in a few minutes. You can just wait here if you want." Margaret smiled. "You're with your usual cabin. And Jason isn't here yet, but he'll be here by campfire."

"Yeah, I knew Jase had something at the University of Georgia."

"Part of growing up." Margaret grinned. "It's what we want for every camper here."

Campers began to show up at the flagpole. Davis reveled in being able to watch all of camp congregate, from the baby campers who were seven to the seniors like him. There were little ones that had bald heads or walked on crutches from new surgeries. There were older campers who looked like they'd never been sick a day in their life.

But he was looking for one camper in particular.

Where was Cason?

"Glad you could show up, loser." Noah bumped into him.

"I like to make an entrance." Davis hugged Grant, one of his counselors, and then the other counselor.

"Because of your need to be the center of attention, you get the top bunk. Sorry," Javier, one of his cabinmates, said. He was a year older than Davis and had a brain tumor.

"Oh, come on." Davis whined. "Jase is going to be later than me. And he's just swimming."

"When you're an elite swimmer, you can have a regular bunk," Grant said.

Campers continued to trickle in, but he still hadn't seen Cason.

He wanted to be there when she got there. He knew

Mari and the other girls in her cabin would take care of making sure she was okay, but still.

It was Cason.

Even if they were just friends, he'd wanted to be there for her.

"She's fine," Noah told him. Not teasing or even giving him a hard time. "I saw her walking up the path with Mari and Paige."

"Oh, are we discussing the new camper in Heather's cabin?" Grant asked, mischief evident in the crinkle of his eyes. Or it could have been that his red hair made him always look like he was up to something.

"Cason is a friend from the hospital." Davis didn't want to get into the drama that had been his life lately.

"By the way, her mom let us know just how good of a friend she is." Grant slung his arm around him. "I promised her I'd have both my eyes on you."

"He said this while pelting Zoie with water balloons," Javier added. "I'm not sure if she took him seriously or not."

And then there she was.

Cason was on her bright-purple forearm crutches, walking up the path with her friends. She was laughing at something one of her counselors said, and happiness sort of radiated off her. It lit that spark of hope in Davis, filling his chest and pulsing out to his fingertips.

Home had never felt so good.

chapter Forty-Five

She finally saw Davis at the flag lowering. Their cabin managed to make it to the lowering early, a miracle according to both Tiny and Heather, her new cabin counselors. Davis was waiting for them, standing with a group of four other guys—his cabinmates, she assumed.

Her cabin had two counselors: Tiny (who was easily over six feet tall) and Heather. Mari was in her cabin, as well as two other girls, Mary Faith Garcia, who went by MF, and Paige. MF was small, appearing to be about twelve when she was close to seventeen. Paige, on the other hand, looked like she'd never been sick a day in her life.

"Where's Jase?" Cason asked Mari. She hadn't seen him when everyone else arrived.

"He'll be here later." She smiled. "He had a swim meet this morning."

"What she's not saying is her boyfriend is an Olympic-level swimmer," Noah interrupted. "Jase won't tell you either."

"Hi." Davis stood close, nearly touching her. "Sorry I wasn't here when you got here."

"I only thought of leaving about fifty times." She laughed, but it was easier to be here now that she'd seen him. She didn't bother to examine whatever that might mean.

"I talked her down," Mari assured. "Glad you're here, jerkface." She hugged him.

"I think Margaret wants our attention." Davis moved closer to Cason, still not touching her. There was a thump to her heart she didn't quite understand.

"Each year at Camp Chemo, we celebrate all of you," Margaret said, pulling Cason from her thoughts. "We also remember the campers we lost over the year. It is our duty to help carry on their legacies. Each camper left a mark here. They were fearless in big ways and small. We want each of you to find ways to be fearless this week."

Cason watched the campers who were circled around the flagpole. There was a warmth from Davis's body, electricity between their bare arms, which were almost touching. Goosebumps rose on her skin, a combination of the proximity of Davis, the others, and the enormity of what was happening around her.

Cason didn't know what kind of mark she would leave on camp, but she was beginning to understand the mark that it would leave on her.

~

"So, we should plan our attack for the X-Games," Heather said as the group walked toward the ball field.

Her voice dropped, and she sounded like a war general who was out in enemy territory.

"Heather, it's a game, not a battle for the universe," Mari laughed.

"So you say," Tiny argued. "If we win, we get to spend the whole week gloating."

"Pride is not a good look for you," Paige quipped. "Besides, we always let the baby campers win."

"It's 'cause they're cute." Heather sighed. "Why can't you guys be cute?"

"Jase thinks I'm cute." Mari smiled and everyone else groaned.

"But seven-year-olds are cute like puppies. And most of them are bald. We can't compete with that." MF sighed, looking down the path where the youngest campers were running.

"It's true." Heather sounded truly crestfallen.

"So what's your event of choice?" Cason smiled at Davis, who magically appeared next to her. "I want to make sure to watch."

"I think I'm supposed to keep it a secret." Cason gripped the handles of her crutches, anything to keep from touching him. He was there again, nearly touching her, in her space but not. "I think I've been chosen to help with the egg toss, and I heard something about the over-under relay."

"You know we'll be up against each other for the relay."

"Well, try to lose gracefully." Cason laughed.

"You've been corrupted, and you've only been here a few hours." The creases around his brown eyes and the way his mouth tilted up at the sides with full abandonment filled her heart with happiness. This was Davis in his true element.

"Where are your friends?" She looked out over his shoulder to the field where various groups of campers began to gather.

"Practicing." He pointed to the entrance to the field, where a group of five guys stood in the way of everyone else trying to enter. They were doing rudimentary stretches and muscle poses. "I'll see you. I should go join them." He let her go before they could get called out for being too friendly with one another, and he hiked up the socks he was wearing to mid-calf before striking his own poses. Cason laughed as her cabinmates joined her, and instead of walking around the boys, just pushed through.

"ARE YOU READY?" roared through a megaphone as the groups gathered around. Cason felt excitement bubbling up in her stomach and chest as the ground rumbled with the stomping of feet. She laughed as Heather tied a tie-dyed scarf around her head and smeared blackout under her eyes (forget the fact that the sun was setting soon). Cason saw Grant up at the front, posing like Adonis in front of Margaret. "Obviously, these jokers think they're going to win the X-Games!" The camp cheered and jeered the boys. "First up is the egg toss!"

"It's time to bring out the heavy artillery." Heather pulled the cabin into a huddle.

"What do you mean?" Cason laughed.

"Gloves." Heather handed an egg to Mari and MF. "And don't be wimpy in your throws."

"Isn't this cheating?"

"We're being creative with the rules." Tiny walked over with Cason, there just to give her a little extra balance once the game began. "And we really only want to beat Grant's cabin."

"Aren't we past the boys versus girls stuff?" Cason tried to raise an eyebrow, but they still hadn't grown back.

"Oh, this isn't about genders, it's about the fact that Grant is a terrible winner . . . and loser. I can't live with a week of his gloating," Tiny explained.

"You are going down!" Grant cheered from next to Mari, but before he could say anything else, Mari chucked her egg at him. The egg splattered and ran down his chest. "Sorry, Heather!" Mari called as she walked off. "He deserved it."

The cabins moved through various games.

By the end of the games, Cason was wet, thanks to a water balloon meant for Jase, who had just arrived. There was one more relay left for the older cabins to compete in. And they were tied with two wins each.

"You okay?" Davis smiled at her, but she got the feeling he didn't mean any of it.

"Just wet." She tried to wring out her shirt for effect,

but it had dried just enough to stick to her and nothing else.

"I'll give you my sweatshirt." He reached out, rubbing his fingers over the hem of her shirt. And that stupid, silly touch made her breath catch. Davis lifted his sweatshirt from over his head, pulling his other T-shirt up just enough that she could see a patch of skin just above the waist of his shorts.

And her brain went blank.

"Over-under relay!" Margaret called. "Line up!"

"I promise to go easy on you," Davis teased, handing her his shirt. Cason was still thinking about his closeness, his skin.

"I don't need your charity." She smiled back. She handed her crutches to Davis, balancing as she slid the sweatshirt over her head. Now his smell was everywhere. "I hear Grant is a sore loser. Sorry for his bad attitude tonight."

The relay was easy, just passing a balloon over your head and then under to the next person. The lack of discernable skill needed made it even more intense between the two oldest cabins.

Cason took the balloon from MF and sent it over her head to Paige. Before she knew what was happening, she was going down. Mari tried to grab her, but she slipped too. They were all laughing, the whole cabin in a tangle on the ground.

"Whoops," Mari said. "I didn't mean to make you

fall." They were all fine, no injuries, just a little mud on their butts.

"Why'd you throw it?" Cason finally asked once another cabin had been declared victor. Cason saw that it was Jared's cabin from the hospital.

"Jared needed the win," was all she said.

And Cason understood.

chapter Forty-Six

In front of the old chapel on the camp grounds was a large fire pit. After the games, the youngest campers were dismissed back to their cabins for nighttime meds and snack. The older cabins joined together at the chapel. They sat in a group, cabins meshed together, friends talking. Davis sat next to Cason, his arm resting protectively behind her back. She leaned back just enough to feel him, the warmth of his arm through his sweatshirt.

Margaret stood in front of the fire pit, holding a wooden box that had been painted with the camp's logo and a box of matches.

"Camp is important." The camp grew quiet with those words, as if everyone knew how true they were. "Camp is a time for us to be together as a family. Camp is a time to push yourself to try something new, to do something different, and to just be. Each person here comes with a story." The words burrowed into Cason's heart. "This week, I want to challenge you to be brave, to try new things, to talk to new people, to do something that scares you just a little." The mountains that flanked camp rose behind her dramatically, giving more importance to her words. "Each year, we use the previous year's ashes to light the campfire. It's a way of remembering who we are, where we've come from, and to light the way for where we are going. And each year, the counselors vote on a camper to come and light the fire." She smiled, looking directly at the group where Cason was sitting. "This year, it's Davis Channing."

"Thanks, Margaret." He said it so softly, if Cason hadn't been so close to the front, she wouldn't have heard him. He held the ashes in his hands and stared at them for a second before speaking. "I was shocked when Margaret called to tell me that I'd be doing this." He shuffled his feet a little. "Mostly because I'm not a great example. I'm not what you expect a cancer survivor to be." He finally looked up at the camp, over Cason's head to where a group of younger campers were listening. "I'm a screw-up, and I know it. This time last year, I was coming off three days in jail and had some pretty serious withdrawal sickness. I'd screwed up everything in my life. And the thing was, I was destroying something that all the doctors and nurses had worked really hard to save." He looked to Cason and his group of friends. "So, I'm not the poster child for Camp Chemo. Instead, I'm someone it saved. Twice." He looked at the ashes once again. "We all have something we're afraid of. We all have something we're fighting." He opened the box and let the ashes fly into the wind and onto the kindling.

"The counselors are going to pass out popsicle sticks

and markers. Write out your dreams for this week. Write out what you're scared of. Write out what questions you're struggling with," he explained, "and we're going to toss them into the fire, let them burn. Maybe it'll help you find your strength or answers." He looked at Cason as he spoke. She held her stick tightly, feeling it cut into the palm of her hand.

Smoke filtered around them as Margaret came up and hugged Davis. "Be brave this year, camp. Be fearless." And with that, Davis lit the fire. Cason stared at her stick and marker before quietly writing, through a haze of tears, *Will I dance again?*

chapter Forty-Seven

Arts and Crafts was teeming with kids of all ages, baby campers to teenagers. Kids milled in different areas, making different projects.

"I recommend tie-dying." Davis pointed it to out Cason. They made their way through the crowded space, heading in the door, when Davis felt a hand grab him at the shoulder and pull him back.

"I don't think so." A woman who had a headband with two dancing clovers on her head pulled him to a stop.

"Kennedy," he whined. It was childish, but he really wanted to go with Cason. "I'm a changed man."

"You're still banned, Davis Channing." Her tight, red-orange curls seemed to glow in her fury. He was mostly sure it was all for show, but then again, he'd thought that when he'd been banned in the first place.

Her thick Irish accent came out as she pulled him back through the room, leaving a laughing Cason in his wake. "You were banned for life. You and Jase! I'm still cleaning dye off the floor! I never got it out of my clothes! I've been told it's still on my scalp." She pushed him playfully out the door into the bright sunlight. "I still find glitter stuck to everything I own! You go find something else to do."

Getting kicked out of Arts and Crafts gave Davis an opportunity to roam camp and see it with fresh eyes. He made his way past the fishing docks toward the memorial garden that had been installed when the camp was built. He took a weathered stone from the scattered rocks laid out and turned over and over it in his hand.

For the first time in a year, he took a deep breath.

A few years ago, there had been names painted on the rocks, remembering kids who were gone. He knew he was lucky. This rock could've been him, because of addiction or cancer. For the rest of his life, he would be a survivor, and that held a lot of weight.

He studied the name on the rock. Catie. Faded pink-and-gold butterflies were on one side. He didn't know her, but she had been in this place like he was now.

Davis enjoyed the faint whoosh of the small waterfall in the garden. Fingering the rock once more, he sat it back by the side of the pond.

"Davis?" Jase came out of the forest. "Thought you might head this way."

"Hey, man." Davis smiled at his friend. "Did you get kicked out too?"

"I didn't even try," Jase said. "I knew better."

"Kennedy holds a grudge."

"We did ruin her glitter supplies." Jase picked up a

rock of his own. "But camp glittered for the rest of the week. It was worth it."

"Who ya got?" Davis referred to the pebble in Jase's hands.

"Dustin." There was a football, baseball, and soccer ball painted on the rock. "I knew him."

"You did?" They sat together.

"He was before you, but he was in our cabin."

Davis let that sink in. There had been a guy he'd never known who had been in their cabin. He sometimes forgot that not everyone made it. Cancer killed.

Jase broke the silence. "We're glad you're back. I'm glad I didn't have to paint one of these for you." Jase, his very earnest and trustworthy friend, gave him a serious look. "There was a time that I thought I might."

"Yeah." Davis inhaled deeply. "Me too." They left the rocks, the memories of campers, and walked the path toward the dining hall.

"So, Davis, how exactly do you feel about glitter?" Cason asked once they were all seated at their tables.

"I think it is the herpes of the craft world and should be outlawed," he deadpanned. "Too bad that Kennedy, Arts and Crafts dictator, disagreed with me." They were all laughing, moving toward the dining hall for lunch.

"Davis, just who I was looking for." Margaret smiled but it was a smile that said something was wrong.

"I didn't do it." He immediately defended himself. "I was with Jase. I didn't even get into Arts and Crafts."

"It's not that." Margaret separated him from his friends, moving him off to the side. "No, your parents are on their way here."

Davis felt his stomach turn in on itself, burning and twisting with anxiety. "Why?"

"They said it had something to do with your assault." Margaret comforted him. "Your parents are signing you out now, but said you'll be back in time for the dance tonight."

"Oh." The twisting didn't stop, instead it grinded and ignited into a deep burn. "Okay."

"You can be brave, Davis."

He could.

He just didn't think he wanted to.

chapter Forty-Eight

"Pool time!" Tiny announced loud enough to cause Cason to jump. "Want me to grab your suit?"

"I'm going to wear my clothes and lounge," Cason shrugged. "I know I can get into the water, but I don't know. It's weird."

"No worries." Tiny easily dismissed the problem. "If you want to change when we get there, we'll figure it out."

As they walked into the pool area, Cason felt more confident, each step strong and powerful . . . until a slip of her crutches on wet pavement taught her just how hard the blacktop was. Her arm caught in the clip of her crutch, forcing her knee to take the brunt of the fall.

"Cason!" She was sure it was Mari.

Paige scooped her up under her arms and had her back up from the ground before she'd really had time to process that she'd fallen at all. "Are you okay?"

She stood there for a moment, her heart racing and the endorphin rush making her feel a bit shaky. She quietly took assessment of her body parts. There was a stinging coming from her elbow, and her knee burned with the scrape. "I'm good," she managed, then, taking a cleansing breath, she chuckled. "I've had worse falls from much higher places, but I think this one was scarier than all of them."

"It's the new weight distribution," Mari told her. "You know how to fall when you're dancing, not when you're missing parts."

MF appeared out of nowhere with both Heather and Tiny, all of them out of breath and with worried looks on their faces. "We saw it happen," MF wheezed. "You okay? I should run more. I should not be this out of breath."

"I'm perfect." Cason shook her head at their harried looks. "I'm going to make Kelsey teach me how to fall correctly."

She laughed when she saw Dr. Henderson casually walk into the pool area to talk with her. He didn't look out of place at camp, just different; no lab coat or stethoscope, instead, a polo and tragically ugly golf shorts.

"Yes, I fell." Her brows furrowed. "I'm fine."

"How's your hip?" He didn't even hide the fact that he was there to check her out. "Chemo makes your bones brittle and easier to break. You could have a fracture and not even know it."

"Seriously, I didn't even hit that hard." She showed him her elbow, which was now a lovely purple color, and she was mildly shocked by how bad it looked.

"Be careful." He nudged her shoulder before heading over to the pool to torture Heather a little.

"What'd Dr. H say?" MF sat down and pulled her

towel over her. She pushed a hand through her nearly black hair, getting the excess water out.

"I'm fine." The boys from the other cabin walked into the pool then. "I do see that Noah is here, shirtless, over there in the pool."

"Well, it is his time to be at the pool." MF became incredibly interested in the magazine in front of her. "He still treats me like I'm twelve."

"Oh." Cason hadn't thought about what it must be like for her, to be old enough to drive but still look like a kid.

"Puberty was somewhat stalled out for me." She blew out a hard breath. "Intense chemo will do that, you know."

Cason looked up and watched the other kids in the pool. There were more than just their two cabins, but no one looked like super models (except for Paige, but she didn't count). "He doesn't seem to mind." Noah removed his prosthesis and hopped to the edge of the pool before jumping in. "His surgery is the coolest."

"Right? He won't tell you, but he was weirded out at first." She flipped the magazine's pages, still not looking up. "And he doesn't care what I look like because I'm his friend. That's it."

Cason didn't have the words to comfort MF. Instead, she put an arm around her and squeezed. Cancer left them all scarred, it seemed. Some scars were more visible than others.

"I hear you are displeased with my services." Kelsey dropped into one of the pool chairs. Her face was streaked with sweat and she had her long hair tied up on top of her head, a wrap holding little tendrils off her face. "Took a spill?"

"Is nothing a secret around here?"

"Nothing." Kelsey laughed.

"I fell, Dr. H looked me over and said I'm mostly fine."

"Mostly?"

Cason lifted her sore elbow to show off the glorious purple bruise. "Maybe if *someone* had taught me to fall correctly, this wouldn't be here."

"Well, maybe if you were a little more graceful," Kelsey teased. "I'll put it on our schedule for next week, right under 'Teach Cason to walk on her new bionic leg.' You ready for practice?"

"What?" The abrupt change of conversation threw Cason.

"You know, showing off your skills on the silks to the fine folks here at camp."

"Kelsey, I'm still not—"

Kelsey plowed through, not letting Cason argue. "I was told by every teacher I ever had that I didn't look like a dancer. It didn't stop me." She didn't have a dancers' body. She was feminine, curvy, with round hips and full thighs. "You have the heart of a dancer and that's what is important."

Cason thought about her words. Her dancer's heart hadn't been amputated, just her leg.

chapter Forty-Nine

Fluorescent lights sucked at his eyeballs. He stood in front of a one-way mirror, looking at Ethan who was sitting at a table. He had to know that Davis was there, on the other side. But Ethan never looked away from the detective interrogating him. He smiled politely, answered questions, and lied through his teeth.

The nerves he had developed while leaving camp had only intensified. Davis was certain he was going to throw up any second. He paced in front of the glass, watching his one-time dealer deny that he knew Davis, deny that he'd been with Alexis.

"We know he's lying." Detective Avery stood next to Davis.

"Yeah." It was the only word Davis could say without vomiting.

"He's not going to get out of this."

"Why is he lying?" Davis couldn't talk. Even if Ethan was in the other room, it was like his hand was still around Davis's throat.

"Because he thinks he's going to get out of this. He hasn't even requested an attorney yet."

"He's not, right?" There was a burning in the back of his throat, and for once, it wasn't because he wanted to use.

"No. We've got a really clear-cut case." Detective Avery's voice softened like the officers in those police shows his mom watched. "We just needed you to make an official ID."

"That's him. That's Ethan Finley."

Then Davis couldn't fight it anymore, his stomach rejected everything that was in his system. Years of chemo had taught him to know when he was going to vomit, he found a trash can and retched into it.

It wasn't like when he'd been dope-sick or even when he'd been on treatment. This was a purge that came from his soul. A rejection of whom he used to be.

After he finished, Detective Avery escorted him to one of the interview rooms where Davis's parents waited. His mom already had a clear soda opened for him.

"Oh, Davis." She tucked him under her arm, wiping his clammy face, holding him close.

"You did good," Detective Avery promised. "It's not easy."

"What's next?" His dad asked. "What do you need from us? Do we need an attorney?"

"Dad, you are an attorney," Davis tried to joke, but it never quite got the legs under it.

"There will be a trial, but for now, Ethan will go to

jail." Detective Avery sat on the desk opposite Davis and his family.

"Thanks for getting him." Davis knew this wasn't the end.

"Don't you have somewhere to be?" Detective Avery smiled at him. "Some camp or something?"

"I do," Davis said. "I do."

chapter Fifty

All Cason's cabin could talk about was the camp dance that evening.

She tried to focus on it too. But she knew Davis had left camp, and that was all her brain could really think about.

"Is this sufficiently 1990s?" Mari asked Heather. She was wearing a flannel shirt over some jeans and had rimmed her dark eyes in black eyeliner.

"Yes. I think I wore that outfit," Heather said as she straightened the choker Mari was wearing.

Cason laughed with her friends as they dressed up in their retro gear. The gym was lit like every bad-movie dance scene.

And there was Davis.

His smile-with-a-wink lifted one side of his mouth, and right then, Cason knew that whatever had happened, it was all okay. The happiness that flooded Cason made her feel like she was levitating. She'd almost forgotten how good it felt to just be, not to worry about chemo or surgeries or prosthetic legs.

"Dance?" Davis was tentative, his hands almost reaching for her but never quite touching her.

"Sure." Butterflies filled her stomach, their wings beating in time with the soft beat of the music. Cason lifted her arms, and her crutches caught around her forearms. "Um." It was awkward. What was she supposed to do with them?

"Here." Davis took them from her and laid the crutches down at their feet, still holding onto her arm in case she needed support. "Problem solved."

They didn't move far, just swayed to the slow music. The beating of her heart pulsed and sped up when she realized she could feel his heartbeat as well, moving just as fast. Both of them were nervous, it seemed. Cason closed her eyes, letting her bald head rest under his chin. The light scruff from him not shaving rubbed lightly on her skin.

It was nice.

Being held by Davis was always nice.

"You were gone for a while today. I saw your parents." She didn't know if she could still pry into his life. Were they still that close? Close like they had been when he was in the hospital?

He didn't answer at first, instead he tightened his grip around her waist, bringing her closer, his breath warm against her ear. "I had to go to the police station."

Cason's heart tripled its beat and plummeted to her stomach all at once.

"I'm fine," he assured her, squeezing her a little closer, seeming to want to absorb her. "Detective Avery had Ethan."

"He's in jail now?" She heard the words, but it was the relief that moved down her that surprised her. Cason hadn't realized she had even been worried about this.

"He is."

"Why did you have to go to the police department?" The song was ending, but they didn't separate. Cason wasn't ready to let him go yet.

"Ethan broke the restraining order. He threatened me outside the NA meeting yesterday."

"Are you okay?" She looked up at him. The lack of light in the gym made it hard for her to see his eyes. Cason wanted to touch his face, to feel the slight stubble under her palm, to offer some comfort, but instead, she tightened her grip behind his neck.

"I'm fine." He swallowed, but there was more to be said. Cason could see it on his face, even in the dark. "I have to be honest with you." She could see pain fill his eyes. "I almost used. A few weeks ago. I scored from him and almost used."

"Davis." She said his name over the hurt that poured from her soul.

"I didn't use." He smiled, but it was wobbly and barely hung on. "Margaret called to tell me about opening camp."

"Oh."

"It reminded me what I would be giving up." He

searched her eyes, she could feel the way his gaze was moving over her, taking in every aspect of her. "And I wanted to see you here."

"Are you okay now?"

"I'm here. And I'm glad you're here."

Cason's grip tightened. "I am too."

~

In the cabin that evening, the girls got ready for bed. The calmness of the evening, the sweetness of the night still lingered over them.

"Okay, ladies." Tiny stopped at her bunk with a jar full of slips of paper. "Pull a slip and then answer."

"Really, Tiny? We do this every year," Paige said, reaching her hand in.

"Really." Tiny plopped down on the foot of Cason's bed and gave her one of the slips. "Heather and I will play too."

"If you could live in one place for the rest of your life, where would it be?" Mari started. She was resting at the foot of her bed, her dark hair piled on top of her head. She rolled her eyes and stuffed the question under her pillow. "That's easy." She grinned, her brown eyes shining. "I'd stay here. Camp."

"Why?" Tiny wriggled her yellow-painted toes and then reached down to do some yoga stretch that Cason had seen on TV.

"It's camp," she laughed. Mari looked over at where

Paige was lying on her own bunk and then back to Cason, MF, and Tiny. "Here, I never explain why I don't wear a prosthesis or what one even is."

Cason nodded. "It's my first year and I get that. Camp's a reprieve, for sure."

"How so?" Heather came in and sat on MF's bed, purposefully taking up most of the space.

"I haven't had to explain anything." Cason smiled. "No sympathy smiles."

"No one asks how you're feeling like you might break apart any minute," MF added.

"I never have to explain what it's like to look like everyone else but not fit in." Paige sat up and squeezed her eyes shut for a moment. "At school, I'd sit in the cafeteria and listen to my friends talk, but they were talking about who just broke up, or prom, or something like that, and all I could think was that Jesse was gone."

"Jesse was on chemo with Paige," MF explained to Cason. "They were pretty inseparable."

"Difference being, I responded to chemo the first time, and he didn't." Paige stood up then. Cason could see the agitation in her lithe form, could see the way she had to move. "He died in the middle of eighth grade, and it nearly destroyed me. I would sit in class and hear my classmates talking and wonder why they were still here when he wasn't. I had no one but camp friends then."

"I'd just started working on the floor when Jesse died. It was rough for all of us." Heather spoke from her spot on

MF's bed. Her arms were resting over her face, blocking out the light.

There was a silence, a moment to remember this person whom Cason would never meet. His death had impacted them in ways she wasn't sure she could understand.

"New slip!" MF broke the sadness, pulling hers out from under her pillow and reading aloud. "What's the most embarrassing thing that has ever happened to you?" She thought for a second. "Oh!" Laughter bubbled up in her as she spoke. "At the time, I thought I'd never recover, and I still get a little mortified when I run into this custodian at the hospital." She sat up and ran a hand through her dark hair as bright-pink spots appeared on her cheeks. "I was getting an x-ray and had to strip—chest films and underwires do not mix—then change into a hospital gown. So, I go into the x-ray room and strip naked from the waist up, not a care in the world, my modesty long gone. And out comes the custodian who had been on the other side of the wall carrying the trash and I'm completely bare chested in front of him. He got so flustered, he dropped his garbage and ran out the door."

"I guess it became a xxx-ray room," Heather laughed.

The entire cabin groaned, throwing whatever they could at her.

"Next question!" Tiny demanded through laughter. "Cason! Go! Please go before Heather tries another joke."

Cason looked at her question and groaned at the universe. "What is your dream job?" She rolled over to her back, unable to look at anyone right then. "I was a ballerina." She let her right foot flex, feeling the pull in the still-good muscles on that side. "I was going to dance *Sleeping Beauty*, *Juliet*, and *Giselle*." Her hand floated up and she watched as her fingers found the floating position instantly without thought. "Now I don't know anything other than I get a new leg next week."

"What's your *dream*, Cason?" Tiny took her hand and squeezed.

"I think it's changed." Her eyes closed and she tried to see herself dancing those dances and wearing the famous costumes, but she couldn't. She couldn't see the person she was mere months before. "I think I want to finish chemo. I think that's my dream."

"That's going to happen." MF flipped over and pushed at Heather so she could see Cason. "That's not a dream, it's a reality."

"Just not my current reality." She knew it wasn't the long-term goal they were thinking of when this question had been written, but it was really all she could think of right then.

"What about still dancing?" Mari stood and crutched through the cabin to where they had a rubber bin full of contraband candy and sodas. "You might not be the ballerina on toe shoes you were, but you can still dance. I saw a documentary on a group of dancers who use wheelchairs. You could come up with something."

"Or it doesn't have to be dance at all." Paige took the

cup Mari offered while she talked. "You could look at this as an opportunity to find something new. Who knows, maybe you're also really good at math or something."

"I think what they're saying is that your dream should be independent of chemo, surgeries, and the fact that cancer is now part of your life." Tiny laid back on Cason's bed, her head level with Cason's. She smiled at her and patted her knee. "It's only a moment for you, not a stopping point."

"Yeah, I wanted to finish chemo, but I still wanted to go to Harvard." MF caught the piece of candy Tiny lobbed at her. "I have to work harder than others. Harvard doesn't take cancer as an excuse for bad grades."

"But, it does make your extracurricular look amazing." Paige joked. "So, Cason, if you could have any dream right now, what would it be?"

"To dance." It was the first time she'd said the words aloud. The words seemed to echo off the walls of the cabin, filling all of the empty spaces with their quiet persistence.

"Then do it," Mari softly replied.

chapter Fifty-one

Davis sat on the floor of his cabin. They were all seated around a cooler, Uno cards in everyone's hands. Grant was currently holding half the deck. Davis was sure Grant was doing it on purpose.

"How was the meet?" Noah asked Jase as he played a blue three, changing the color from yellow.

"I kept my title. But I'm glad that part of my life is officially over."

"You're not swimming in college?" Javi asked. He pulled his cap lower over his head. His dark hair had never grown all the way in after his cranial radiation.

"No, I'm retired." Jase played a reverse, sending it back to Davis and forcing him to draw several cards before Davis could finally lay down a playable one.

"A retiree at eighteen," Grant teased. "You moving into the assisted living soon?"

"Just Brumby." Jase named his future dorm. "Javi, where are you going again?"

"Uh," he paused and then his cheeks heated, "Northwestern." The game stopped as they stared at their friend. It was no surprise that Javi was smart, but this was news. "I know! I was all set to go to Tech and let Mari's parents feed me, but the offer from Northwestern was too good."

"That's awesome!" Noah crowed. "You big nerd."

"Are you nervous?" Davis asked.

"A little, I mean, I still have a brain tumor. Mine's not going anywhere." Javi blew out a breath. "And I'll have to be scanned there like I am here, but it's not like Chicago doesn't have a pretty decent medical system."

"And your parents?" Grant asked, playing a draw four before changing the color to green. Jase groaned as he drew the cards, since he'd almost been out, but he didn't complain too much.

"That took a little more persuading. Mom is still not completely on board. And I think she keeps hoping I'll change my mind. But MF's parents talked with them."

"Doctors Garcia are pretty convincing."

"Yeah, they're the reason I got to come to camp at all," Javi laughed. "Not speaking a lot of English, having a son with a brain tumor . . ." He trailed off. "I can see why my parents are nervous."

"Yeah, it's a long way from home." Davis hadn't even allowed himself to think of leaving the state. "If I'm honest, being that far from home kind of terrifies me." He played a card, but didn't have any strategy going on. "I'm nervous about college."

"Why?" Grant asked. He had on his doctor face, the one that meant he was listening and ready to help.

"Lots of temptation around," Davis breathed. "Going to college when you're in recovery is trickier. Sometimes my sobriety is second-to-second and being around that much stuff . . ." He trailed off, staring at his cards, unable to look his friends in the eyes.

"I think it says something that you're even thinking about that." Noah's brow furrowed. "And you've still got another year before you go."

"A lot can happen in a year," Davis agreed, but he didn't elaborate how a lot could happen in either direction.

"Voilà!" Grant laid his last card, going out in a grand gesture. "You guys thought I was never going to win! You were so busy talking you didn't even notice that I called Uno."

"What were you doing?" Davis laughed incredulously. "Stockpiling draw fours?"

"Skill." Grant stood, stretching and flexing his muscles. "Lots of skill."

"Whatever." Jase tossed his cards down on top of the cooler. Each of the guys stood, stretched, and moved to their respective bunks. The cabin was still sort of clean, no boxers hanging from the rafters like there would be by the end of the week.

"Hey, Davis?" Grant moved over to his top bunk.

"Yeah?"

"Don't let your past dictate your future. Okay?" Grant offered. "I know it seems scary and overwhelming right now, but you can find support on campus and new meetings."

"Thanks. I hadn't thought that far ahead."

"Don't limit yourself."

"Right." Davis didn't pry into Grant's life, but he got the feeling that Grant understood exactly what he was feeling. He was sharing something with Davis that he wouldn't share with others.

"Also, don't think I didn't notice that extra-long slow dance." Grant glared teasingly. "I've got both my eyes on you, Channing."

chapter Fifty-Two

The words *be brave* filled Cason's brain.

She could do this.

Billowing silks dripped down from the rafters of the stage. It was like everyone around her was conspiring for her to perform. Cason stood just off stage right, an arm's length away from the silk. All she had to do was take one step and she could touch them.

Perform.

Just thinking the word hurt.

She stepped in, her fingers rubbing the soft fabric, holding it almost like it was fragile.

These silks could help her dance.

Could help her perform.

Cason could be as brave as Davis and do the thing that scared her the most.

"Hey!" Kelsey bounced over to where Cason stood, shocking her. She dropped the silk like it was made of fire. "What's up?"

The words were in her throat, bubbling to be said, nearly painful in their urgency, but fear was just as strong.

Fear could hurt just as much. Fear was dripping over her silence.

"I want to be brave." Cason cleared her throat. She couldn't say the words. She couldn't get them around the fear.

"Okay." Kelsey tucked Cason in, bringing her close. "Let's be brave."

Together, they started moving in the silks, climbing up higher, attempting more difficult poses, finding ways for Cason to dance within the weight and holds.

The silks were a comforting partner.

"Time," Kelsey panted as she slid down and out of the silk, helping Cason do the same. "I've got some campers waiting." Cason looked out and a gaggle of little girls were watching.

"I want to dance like that." A little girl peeked out from behind her counselor, her bright-silver crutches up under her arms. "I could do that."

Cason felt unexpected tears fill her eyes. She had danced and this little girl saw it. Even the youngest of campers could tell that Cason was a dancer.

Kelsey pulled Cason close. "What are you thinking now?"

"I need to perform." Fear be damned.

~

Cason was exhausted from her work that day in the silks, but here she was in the treehouse with her cabin and the rest of her team. It was Capture the Flag, and Mari would never forgive her if she tried to get out of it.

"Who has a plan?" Mari was pacing along the treehouse, her crutches making a clacking sound with each step.

"Uh, get the flag?" Joel, one of the other guy campers called out. "Isn't that the point?"

Mari narrowed her eyes at him, barely suppressing a grin. "Okay, turd, you're on cage duty."

"Mari, we lose every year, and we're gonna lose again this year." Joel looked around the group. "What? With Davis back, they'll be unstoppable."

"We lost last year and he wasn't even here," another camper spoke up.

Mari pulled at the knot of curls on top of her head and sat down on the floor with a thud, her crutches crashing behind her. "This is so stressful."

"What about if we just attack?" Tiny suggested. "Like, sure, most of us will get sent back to base, but maybe someone could get through."

"Didn't we try that a couple years ago?" Paige handed Mari a piece of candy. "I tried to get intel, but they found me."

"Ugh." Mari laid down on the floor with obvious frustration, biting off the red licorice.

"Wait," Cason spoke up. "I have an idea."

chapter Fifty-Three

Davis and Jase slid climbing harnesses around their waists and climbed the ladder up the back of the climbing wall to hang their flag. They never actually climbed the wall, just made it look like they did.

"The other team always thinks that we climb the wall," Jase said.

"You would think they'd realize we use the ladder around back." Davis pulled his harness, straightening it. "I'm starting to feel bad about it."

"Don't," Jase groaned. "If Mari's team ever won, we would never hear the end of it."

"Mari?" Cason's voice called. She sounded lost.

"Cason?" Davis smiled as she came into his view.

In slow motion, Davis watched as Cason turned, screamed in fright, and then tumbled to the ground. Her crutches went everywhere, her body landed with a thud.

Davis was at her side, moving dirt off her knee where she hit. "Are you okay?"

"You scared me," she sniffled. "I lost the group when we split up to ambush you guys."

"Are they ever going to try a new tactic?" Jase came over to her. "Anything hurt?"

"My knee." She blinked away tears. "I think it's bruised."

"You should go find someone," Davis instructed Jase. He could feel his heart pounding in his throat, thinking only the worst.

"Please?" Cason sniffed again. "I think Heather is out there somewhere." Davis pulled her close, tucking her fragile form against his body. Jase ran out through the woods, looking for someone to help them. Davis hoped nothing was broken, that it had been only the fall that had shaken her.

"It doesn't look too bad." Davis pulled back to look at her knee again. "I'm sure it's nothing."

"Hey!" He heard Jase yell. "They've got the flag!" Paige took off, running through the others as his team attempted to catch her, but her head start made it impossible.

Mari stood there with her hands on her hips, her crutches framing her body. "I figured out that you use the ladder."

"It's about time," Jase laughed as they walked through the woods back toward the main part of camp.

"You know what?" Cason smiled demurely. "I'm feeling all sorts of better now. Thanks."

"Victory!" MF shouted as she ran through the woods past them. Davis just sat there, frozen by the very clever play Cason had made.

"You won this round, Martin," he stood, brushing himself off, "but just wait."

"I'm terrified." She stopped, the sound of the horn letting everyone know that the game was over. "You can see I'm shaking in my shoe."

"Next year, sweetheart."

"We'll see," she challenged. Cason crossed back to Davis, getting in his personal space and filling it up. Everyone seemed to have scattered and they were alone in the woods. "You're just mad that we won."

"I'm impressed with your ability to go along with this plan." He didn't stop himself this time, but wrapped his arms around her, pulling her to him. "Your cabinmates have turned you to the dark side so easily."

"Oh," her breath was hot on his neck, "this was all my idea."

Davis laughed uproariously. He held her close before lifting her off the ground, swinging her around in delight. Her crutches swung out from her sides like wings as they circled, and he gently sat her back down to hold her tight.

She looked up at him with large eyes that crinkled at the sides with her smile.

Davis leaned forward and let his mouth brush over hers. He wanted to make sure she wanted this, that she wouldn't pull away. She didn't pull away. Taking the kiss deeper, he held her closer, his hand against the small of her back. There was a pounding in his chest, and he couldn't be sure if it was his heart or hers.

"I'm very glad to be here," Cason laughed.

"I'm very glad that you are here." He still had her close, not willing to let her go, to pull away. Cason still had her arms around his neck with her fingers laced together. Her crutches were resting against his back, but he didn't mind.

"You're pretty great, you know?" Cason said as her smile broadened, her mouth close to his.

"You know, I am in the running for the world's greatest boyfriend."

She stared up into his face, barely visible under the moonlight in the woods. "Is that what you are?"

"The world's greatest boyfriend?" His heart stopped for a second. "I guess that's up to you." He tilted her chin up, their mouths nearly touching.

"My boyfriend." A smile moved across her face, filling his heart. "I'd like that." His thumb slid over her cheekbone, bringing them even closer. Kissing her again was the simplest thing he'd ever done.

chapter Fifty-Four

The last full day of camp always came too quickly. "I'm going to stop by the garden," Davis told Grant before trotting off toward the quiet little oasis in camp.

The gentle sounds of the small waterfall met him before he got to the actual garden. Sitting down, he pulled out the chip that was in his pocket.

One year.

Today he was one whole year sober.

With the scattering of rocks around, he studied the names of campers who had come and gone before him. There was Dustin's right where Jase had left it. A bright-pink one with a huge daisy had "Ashley" scrawled across the top. More and more rocks, there were probably at least a hundred. That meant that someone had sat and painted each of these with small memories of people. Small tokens of remembrance covered the place.

"Hey." Cason, nearly silent despite her crutches, came toward him.

"Hi." Davis looked up at her. "I needed a moment of quiet."

"Camp doesn't have a ton of those, does it?"

He helped her sit, taking her crutches and laying them down. "Not particularly."

"What's that?" She motioned to his chip.

"It's my one-year-sober chip." He smiled at her. "Today's the day."

"Today?" Her smile spread slowly across her face, taking up most of it with a pure joy. "That's a pretty big deal, Davis Channing."

"It is," Davis agreed readily, laughing a bit. "I definitely didn't think I'd be here a year ago." He flipped the chip between his fingers. "Hell, a couple weeks ago I didn't think I'd be here."

"What did you think?"

He glanced up from the token to his girlfriend. "That I didn't want to be in that place anymore."

"You've come pretty far." Cason reached out and gripped his hand, the coin held between them.

He studied their fingers, hers small and delicate between his thicker ones. "I was, I don't know . . . lost."

"But you're not, now."

"No." There was a pause as he looked for his words. "I wander sometimes, but I'm not lost."

She smiled before placing a soft kiss on his lips. "Congrats, Davis. There's a lot of hard work in that little chip." She traced a finger over the name on a nearby rock, "Jesse," before picking it up and looking at the cross that was on the other side. "Davis, you've done something great this year." She put the rock down before looking at him.

"The pull is still there. And I'm not sure it will ever go away, but being here," he breathed in, taking in his surroundings and his heart, "makes it easier to remember why I do this."

"Congratulations, Davis." She kissed him. "You've done the remarkable."

chapter Fifty-Five

"Are you ready to be remarkable?" Kelsey whispered into her ear as they stood right off the wooden stage while Margaret introduced the last campfire. Kelsey usually had a couple of her groups from the week perform, but this year it was only Cason.

"Sure." She nodded. The butterflies in her stomach were dancing a Russian troika, and she wasn't sure if it was because she was dancing or because she was dancing in front of the entire camp. But there it was, nerves. She offered Kelsey a lame smile, and then ran both hands over her head, no longer shocked to find it completely bald.

"You need sparkles." Heather came out of nowhere and all but bathed Cason in glitter before she could protest. "Sparkles are for courage and just being brave." She hugged Cason. "You're amazing. I'm so proud of you."

"Go," Kelsey pointed. "How can you see her dance if you're back here?"

"Thanks." Cason took a minute to collect herself. "Who knew there could be people more smothering than my mom?"

"It's her job." Kelsey smiled. "Ready? 'Cause you're up."

This time, Cason's smile was real, and while the troika was going strong, her own excitement outweighed it. There were no fancy curtains or lights like she was used to, just a barnlike stage in front of old, slatted benches. Some can lights lit the stage, barely giving off enough light for the audience to see. Cason knew that this would be the best audience she had ever danced in front of. Everyone here, her friends, counselors, even her doctor, wanted to see her succeed.

And then there was Davis. She could just barely make him out as she crutched onto the stage and got into position. She knew he was there, could feel his gaze over everyone else's. She wrapped the silk around one arm and Kelsey took her crutches, laying them out of the dance space.

The faint chords of Tchaikovsky's *Sleeping Beauty* flowed from the speakers, and Cason was on. The silks allowed her to move, to pull herself through the air and to bend her body in shapes that she'd only dreamed of since her diagnosis. She moved from an inverted *arabesque* to a split, the silk cradling her residual limb like a swing, the silks splayed below her like she had the giant wings of a butterfly. Glancing out, she heard a tiny gasp as she pulled her body upright, standing in the silk. She twisted as if to do a *pirouette* and then dropped down, her residual limb acting as her anchor.

Her fingers floated and her arms were poised in motion as she let her body take over and the music lead her.

She was lost in the world that she had so desperately missed.

And she was found.

She was dancing.

She looked briefly off the stage, catching Kelsey's eye, as she slid back into a bend. The silks wrapped around her waist and hips like a cradle as she came to the last position. She floated as she came down from the silks.

She stood to bow, the entire camp cheering and clapping, and before she even came back up, she was crushed by the hugs of her friends and counselors.

When they finally parted, Davis stood back, waiting. She hurried to him, and he pulled her close, holding her tight. "You danced." The words were whispered thickly into her ear.

Cason smiled up at him, her eyes glowing with happiness and excitement. "I danced." Relief and joy pulsed in time with every beat of her heart. She looked out over her the crowd of friends, the people who walked her right back into dance and felt her heart soar. "I danced!"

"Cason, that was beautiful."

She turned around at the voice. "Mom!" She threw herself into her mother's waiting embrace. "What are you doing here?"

"Heather called and said I could come watch." Her mother hugged her again, wrapping her in another tight embrace. "You were gorgeous."

"I don't have to go home now, do I?"

"Not until tomorrow." She wiped at her face.

"We'll let you two talk for a bit." Heather hugged Cason as she moved the group of friends away. "I'll wait for you over by the snack shack."

"What did you think?" Cason sat down on the lip of the stage, and Natalie slid up next to her.

"I think that you are still one of the best dancers in the nation."

"I'm glad I didn't know you were coming," she confessed. "My extension is lacking."

"Cason, your extension has always been perfect." She pulled her toward her. "I've always been too hard on you," Natalie smiled softly. "I've always wanted you to be the best."

"I wanted to be the best."

"And you are," Natalie promised. "I loved getting to watch you up there." She kissed the top of Cason's bald head. "You were so graceful. It was like you had been doing this your entire life."

"I have." Cason slowly smiled. "I'm always going to be a dancer."

"I will always love what you do, Cason." She hugged her closer. "Always."

"Thanks, Mom."

"I love you."

"I love you too." They talked for a bit longer. Natalie let her know that she would be back the next day to get her.

Then her mom smiled, a little mischief in her eyes. "Don't think because you did something remarkable that the camp rules don't apply. I'm going to check and make sure those counselors keep a close eye on that boyfriend of yours."

Heat filled Cason's cheeks, but she just smiled again. Because, standing just behind her mother, waiting on her, was Davis. He waved at her mom as she left the amphitheater, and the two of them were alone.

Davis didn't hesitate as he wrapped her in his arms. She breathed in deeply, still infatuated by his scent. They were no longer the same people they had been before camp. Davis seemed calmer somehow, more settled in himself. And she remembered how angry and fearful she had been. She couldn't say that camp had made all those feelings go away, but she could say that she no longer felt confined by the crutches and a new prosthesis.

Together, they started to walk away from the amphitheater toward the chapel where the older half of camp waited. Davis held onto her arm just above her elbow, keeping their connection.

Cason glanced back at the stage, looking at the billowing silks one last time.

She had not just danced.

She had flown.

Author's Note

When I was a teenager and reading every book I could get my hands on, I was desperate for a girl who looked like me. For a girl who had cancer and lived. And it was really hard to come by. So, I wrote one.

In late February of 1989, I was diagnosed with Ewing's Sarcoma. Just like Cason. I had my left leg amputated. Like Cason. But, that's really about the only places our stories are similar. I was only eight at diagnosis and amputation. And no cute boy who volunteered ever danced with me while I was getting chemo. A boy did steal my sparkly shoelace for a scavenger hunt around the hospital (looking at you, Danny), but like I said, I was eight. I've lived most of my life as a cancer survivor and a disabled person.

I was treated at Children's Healthcare of Atlanta at the Egleston Campus. My wing was 3 North B, and I had the best team of doctors and nurses looking out for me. They cared not only about me medically, but emotionally as well. I always knew I could tell them anything. People like Dr. Henderson and Heather are fictional, but they have real-life counterparts and they are responsible for the adult I am.

I was lucky that my hospital was affiliated with Camp Sunshine. Camp is one of my favorite places on this earth. I have always felt so lucky that I got to spend a week with other kids who had cancer. Like the girls talk about in their cabin chat, not having to explain what it was like to someone, was so meaningful to me as a young adult. Now I continue to volunteer as a cabin counselor, and spending a week with group full of campers is one of the most rewarding things I get to do. There are camps for kids and teens with cancer all over the country. And I'm not being hyperbolic when I say they're life-saving.

Childhood cancer has better survival rates right now than it ever has. But, it is still the number one disease killer of children and adolescents. It is also severely un-derfunded. The NIH currently only offers 4% of its budget to research and the development of better treatments for childhood cancers. There are diseases that only children are diagnosed with that still have a 0% survival rate. And if we are lucky enough to survive, 80% of childhood cancer survivors live with life-impacting, long-term side effects including heart failure, secondary cancers, and fertility problems.

But, we live. And we live great lives.

To find out more about the oncology camps in your area, visit the Children's Oncology Camping Association. www.cocai.org

To find out more information about Camp Sunshine, please visit www.mycampsunshine.com. (This is for Camp Sunshine in Georgia.)

To find out more information about the Aflac Cancer and Blood Disorders Center at Children's Healthcare of Atlanta, please visit www.choa.org/cancer.

To make a donation directly to an organization that funds only childhood cancer research, please visit www.curechildhoodcancer.org.

Acknowledgments

"For I know the plans I have for you," declares the Lord, "plans to prosper you and not to harm you, plans to give you hope and a future." –Jeremiah 29:11

I have to thank Jason, my loving and patient husband. You have given me the time and love to write stories that sometimes make me worthless. Thank you for loving me and for understanding when I ask you to pick up dinner again.

Kennedy and Eleanor, thank you so much for being patient with Mama as she worked. Thank you for understanding when I said, "just one more minute." And not complaining (too much) that I was still working on the book.

To the formidable and talented McKelle George and Carlisa Cramer. Friends, I can never ever ever thank you for turning *Brave Enough* into what is here. Thank you for asking for more camp, because you got camp. McKelle, thank you for never giving up on this story.

To Mari Kesselring, seriously. Thank you for believing in my story, for getting why it needed to be told, and for appreciating fine glittery stationery.

Eric Smith, you have believed in every word I've written. You have guided me through countless changes, hits and misses, and every other thing publishing can throw at a person. Thank you for being. And Nena and Langston, thank you too. I know who holds it all together.

My family, I wanted to list each of you by name, but I'm so lucky that I have a large and loving family. Thank you for loving me, holding my hand through the years, and reminding me that Mama wanted me to create.

To Jenn Foster, Jennifer Davis, Elizabeth Riley, and my FBP/FBR family, thank you for being encouraging and loving and telling me that it will get done.

To Stacy Criscione, Amy Freed, Elise VanderMeer, and Anne Mitchell, thank you for being the best friends a new mom could have. And encouraging me to take time to write.

Katie Morgan and Emily Grace Blackstone, thank you for reading my terrible General Hospital FanFic and becoming trusted friends. Heather Neal, thank you for asking for chapters of *Brave Enough* for your birthday to help me put words on a page, chapter 30 is for you.

To Katherine Locke, thank you for taking a rough and weary manuscript and helping me craft it into a real book. You will see your work all over this.

To Team Rocks, thanks for the conversation, holding my hand, and reminding me not to chase waterfalls, especially if they might be filled with glory.

Lucky 13, Rebecca Caprara, Julie Dao. Mara Fitzgerald,

Austin Gilkerson, Heather Kaczynski, Jessica Rubinkowski, Jordan Villegas, and Kevin VanWhye. Thank you for being some of the first friends I had in publishing.

To MadCap Retreats, thanks for reminding me that I'm a storyteller and that I have infinite stories to tell.

Rebecca Caprara and Jessica Whalon, thank you for your expertise and reading through my novel to make sure it was accurate and a thoughtful portrayal.

Mary Dunbar and Rachel Meridee, thank you for being the best CP's a girl could ask for. Thank you for reading every incarnation of this book and always giving me truthful feedback. Tia Bearden and Kristen Walters, thank you for your love and support during these last few rounds of edits.

To my very own Dr. H, Dr. Roger Vega. You guided me through one of the scariest things I've ever done. You've held my hand at every major life event I've had. I know you give this to all your patients, but I've always felt like it was just for me.

To Camp Sunshine, staff and counselors, thank you for making a place that could save a kid from the realness of cancer. Bubbles, thank you for the glitter. To Kristine Rudolph, who told me to write a camp story.

To my Camp Sunshine Posse, Sarah, Talley, Kelly, Hayley, Erin, Emily, and so many others, thank you for being my friends. For giving me memories that fueled the other fifty-one weeks out of the year.

To my campers past, present, and future. This is a

work of fiction. There is no kissing at camp. That never happens despite what I've written. I think y'all are all neat.

And to the people who walked this earth for too short of a time. To Katie Cleveland, Dustin Dove, Jesse Smith, Lee Veach, Chad Autry, Erik Kittico, Dave Byrd (thanks for loaning me your smile with a wink), Catie Wilkins, Jack Williamson, Jon Allmett, and too many others. Sunshine Forever, Baby. Sunshine Forever.